TERRY FOSS

BEOTHUK SLAVES

Terry Foss

Published by: Fossil

4 Harvard Drive

Mount Pearl, Newfoundland and Labrador,

Canada

A1N 2Z7

ISBN 978-0994020987

Published October 2020

Printed in United States

Edited by: Cathy Anstey

Cover Art: Claude Randell

Terry's Books

Beothuk Slaves

Bloody Point

Red Indian - The Beginning

Red Indian - The Final Days

Red Indian - The Early Years

Dedication

This book is dedicated to the many Beothuk who were captured and torn from their home, taken to a strange land, forced to live in a strange culture and serve an unsympathetic master, never to find their way back home.

This book will help us to remember you.

Preface

Gasper Corte Real was born into a family of explorers in the kingdom of Portugal in 1450. He was the youngest of three sons and accompanied his father, Joao Vaz Corte-Real on his expeditions to North America.

Joao Vaz Corte-Real was governor of the island of Terceira in the Azores, located almost halfway between Portugal and Newfoundland.

As was the custom in these times, young nobles completed their education living with high born nobility, and so Gaspar and his brothers spent much of their youth in the royal court. In 1500 he was sent by King Manuel I to find a Northwest passage to Asia. Reaching Greenland, he was unable to land because of heavy ice, and was forced to return to Portugal. The next year he set out again, accompanied by his brother Miguel, and encountering frozen seas he turned south.

It is believed he then landed on the coast of Newfoundland somewhere in the Notre Dame Bay area.

This is where our story begins....

1

Two things would change Paublo's life, neither of which he would understand until later. The first a chance meeting, the second his decision to go to sea.

Born as an only child to a farmer, he had been taught to love the soil and all it could produce, yet he had always been restless and at an early age felt the draw of the sea. The fields his father had been given to work on their island home of Terceira covered a gently sloping hill and had an unobstructed view of the harbour and the ocean beyond. From there, he got to see every ship that entered the harbour. He never failed to stop what he was doing in the field and watch those grand sailing ships with a mixture of envy and an overwhelming longing to stand on their decks and feel the wind in his face. He doubted it would ever happen, but still he dreamed. For now, it was all he had.

His father quietly watched what was happening. In his heart he knew the day would come when he would be watching one of those grand ships leaving the harbour carrying his only son. His mother fervently prayed the fascination would pass and he would stay safely on land where she could watch over him. That's how it's supposed to be, she reasoned with God. He needs me and I need him.

Tomorrow was his birthday. The past sixteen years had gone too quickly. She wished her boy was still a toddler. Then she could tell him no, and that would be the end of it. But he wasn't, and she couldn't.

Looking through the open door, she watched Paublo emerge from the weather-scarred barn, chicken scattering from his path in alarm. He was such a good-looking boy. She smiled with pride as she stepped onto the bridge, leaned her shoulder against the veranda post and called his name.

His broad smile, as he lifted his head and acknowledged her, warmed her heart. She thought she would never get tired of that. She hoped she would never have to. The familiar overpowering urge to fold him in her arms and hug him washed over her as he approached the porch steps, but with great effort she restrained herself. He was no longer comfortable with her open display of affection. She knew it was not a reflection of his feelings, simply the manifestation of a growing boy who was all too quickly approaching manhood.

"Paublo, I need you to go down to the docks and fetch a fresh fish," she said. "Tomorrow is your birthday and I want to make something special."

"OK Mother," he said, as she retrieved several coins from her stained apron pocket and dropped them into his outstretched hand. She gently folded his fingers over the coins.

"Tell Father where I've gone," he said.

"I will," she said, as she watched him walk through the gate and follow the winding footpath that would take him to the docks at the seashore.

Paublo whistled as he walked, no particular tune, at least not that he knew. He didn't have his mother's gift for music, probably more like his father. He couldn't sing either. Not being able to sometimes frustrated him. He whistled. It was something he had begun to do lately. He wasn't sure how it happened. It just felt right.

This was going to be a special occasion for sure. He knew his parents had little money, and to spend what they had on a fish for him had to be a sacrifice. This was going to be a great birthday. If only his present could be a berth on one of those great ships. He clutched the coins tightly in his right hand deep inside his trouser pocket as he picked his way along the rock-strewn path.

2

Several makeshift stalls had been built along the shoreline where the fishermen peddled their wares. Their small boats were tied to wharfs that jutted into the water only short distances from the beach, unlike the larger wharf that extended much further into deeper water for the ocean-going ships.

He had strolled the length of the big wharf before but had never paid much attention to the small ones used by the village fishermen. He had no interest in them. It was the ocean that drew him, the promise of adventure and visiting other lands, some that had never been visited before. The water travelled by the local fishermen was too close to the land he was all too familiar with.

He had stopped whistling some time ago.

He approached the first stall and waited patiently as the owner sorted fish from several tubs, back on to him. The smell of fish was strong where he waited, but not enough to mask the smell of the sea brought to him by the light onshore breeze. He drew in deeply through his nostrils. He somehow knew his destiny was out there somewhere on the ocean.

Straightening up, the owner pulled the wool cap off, letting long red hair tumble free to her shoulders. She rubbed the woolen cap across her damp forehead as if to scratch an annoying itch. Half turning, she noticed him standing there with his elbows resting on the window ledge.

His breath caught and for a moment he completely forgot what he had come for. In fact, his head had drained of almost all thought. Those that remained he could not seem to organize. He thought maybe his mouth had fallen open. He licked his lips, that somehow had suddenly gone dry, to check.

She watched him with a half-smile. "So, what can I do for you this fine day," she finally said. Her voice sounded musical. He himself had no ear for music, but his mother did. He loved to hear her sing. This girl's voice had the same sound. He thought he would like to listen to her sing.

The thumping in his chest was so strong he was sure she could hear it. He knew he had never seen so beautiful a face. The fish-stained apron that hung from her neck to her knees could not take away from it. He knew there were words he needed to say but his confused mind kept dropping them, bumping them up against each other so that they made little sense when strung together. He chose to say nothing.

5

He slid his elbows from the ledge and let his arms fall slackly at his sides. He stepped back. It was as if he was standing in her space uninvited, a place where he shouldn't be. He just nodded with a wide smile framing his face.

"Is it fish you're after?" she asked.

He nodded again. He remembered why he came.

"Well it's fish we've got," she grinned. "Has the cat got your tongue? What's your name?"

"Paublo," he mumbled, not believing he actually spoke it aloud.

"Paublo. That's a nice strong name," she said, with that stunning smile.

He could not take his eyes off her face. He wished he could touch it.

She turned and pulled a large cod fish from one of the tubs, holding it with fingers thrust inside its spread gills. Her long hair had fallen across her face as she bent. Standing erect again, she tossed her head to the side, flicking the hair back over her shoulder where it belonged. Paublo found it hard to breathe, and a tightness squeezed his chest. He had never felt this way before. It seemed as if some of the strength had gone from his legs. He moved back to the window and leaned on the ledge for fear he would fall. He wondered if there was something wrong with him. But then he thought there couldn't be anything wrong if he felt this good.

She hoisted the wet fish and spread it on the window ledge next to him. A bead of water settled on his face as the tail slapped down on the wood. He lifted his hand and absentmindedly wiped it away. The smell lingered.

"Will this one do?" she asked.

As she released the fish her hand brushed his. Sparkes shot up his arm into his chest. He gave a tiny gasp of surprise. She was so close. He had no idea what to do.

He left his hand where it was in the hope she would accidently touch it again.

"That one is good," he said, clearing his throat that had become as dry as the midsummer soil in the sunbaked fields. "I'll take it."

He opened his right hand where he had been fiercely gripping the coins and let them spill onto the window shelf.

She selected several and pushed the rest back to him, letting her hand come to rest next to his.

Staring at her hand, he wondered if she had done it on purpose. No, he thought. Why would she?

He lifted his head and looked into the deep pools of her brown eyes, just above her enchanting smile. He thought he might drown.

Clumsily he picked up the coins and deposited them in the pocket of his trousers. Slipping his fingers into the gills as he had seen her do, he lifted the fish from the window and turned to leave. He was expected back home. Realizing with alarm he didn't know her name, he turned back.

"Maria," she said, as if reading his thoughts. Her laughter was magical. He didn't want to leave, ever. He didn't care if he stood there long enough to grow roots.

"I have to go to the wharf. My father is waiting for me in the boat." she said. "There's fishing to be done."

He nodded with disappointment.

"I will see you around, Paublo," she said as she walked away, her long hair cascading over her shoulders and down her back.

Paublo began to follow the footpath that brought him here, the fish dangling from his right hand, its tail occasionally scraping the ground. He continued to glance over his shoulder from time to time, hoping to catch another glimpse of her, but she had disappeared behind the stalls.

3

A fine mist of salt spray swept down the deck and brushed across Gaspar's face, flung by an early May breeze that curled white caps from the tops of the waves. He smiled with satisfaction as he wrapped his long woolen coat around him and licked the faint taste of salt from his lips. Standing with his feet braced firmly on the deck, he let his hips roll with the motion of the ship. For him it was as natural as riding a well-heeled horse. This was where he felt most at home, with the feel of a strong ship beneath his feet and the North Atlantic wind in his face. He was an explorer, an adventurer, but first of all a seaman. It was in his blood, just as it had been in his father's, just as it was in his older brother, Miguel's, who was standing on the deck of the ship that followed a short distance behind to starboard.

The water had always had a pull on him. As long as he could remember he wanted to be around it. From playing on the beaches on their island home of Terceira and then the shores around Lisbon, to watching his father sail into the distant horizon, desperately yearning to be on the ship with him, to finally being allowed to accompany him. It had always been about the draw of the sea. When he was younger, his mother had told him he had seawater in his veins, and he sometimes wondered if there might just be some of that in there.

Once a year the family had made the two week sail from Terceira in the Azores to Lisbon when his father was summoned to the king's court to give account of the affairs on the island and the results of his excursions abroad. While Miguel and Vasco took this time to play, Gaspar never strayed far from his father's side, watching and learning how to sail the ship, and how to use the charts and stars to find their way.

Five years ago, just before he died, his father had given him all his charts, with his many personal notations scribbled around the edges. Gaspar had spent hours pouring over those maps until he had committed every detail to his memory. They were his most treasured possession and went everywhere he went, providing a lasting connection to his father and his mentor.

Pulling his mind back to the present, he looked past the taut sails of his brother's ship to where he could barely see the entrance to Lisbon harbour in the distance, the detail he was so familiar with fading into a hazy blue outline. He wondered when he would return to see it again. Turning back, he ran a critical eye down the deck and up the rigging, stopping to watch the work of each sailor as they did what was necessary to harness the wind and push the ship toward the island of

Terceira, the first leg of the trip. There, in two weeks time, with favorable winds, he would be joined by the third ship, captained by his friend Antonyo.

It seemed that the sailors were tackling their tasks with enthusiasm, as if they too were glad to be at sea again, to be a part of whatever the voyage had in store for them. Their shouted challenges and jests to each other gave the ship a youthful feel. The mood was infectious. Gaspar smiled with anticipation as he lifted his eyes toward the cloudless sky.

High above him, perched on the crossbar of the main mast, was the last of the gulls which had followed them out of the harbour, the final holdout. In the distance, the tiny white specks that made up its departing companions were disappearing into the blue haze as they returned to the shore. Gaspar watched it as it finally spread its wings in resignation and pushed off in the direction of the disappearing land, marking its departure with a grey white splat that hit the rail a little to his left.

Most of the crew of all three ships had sailed with him and his father on previous explorations. They, like him, were born for the sea and could find little enjoyment when landbound for any extended period of time. They were only happy with the salt wind caressing their faces and the deck rolling beneath their feet. They were good men, familiar with the ships and with their captains, men whom Gaspar would trust with his life.

11

The first two weeks of this voyage was in familiar waters, in fact until they reached the Azores it would feel like the voyage had not started at all. It did, however, represent the halfway mark between Portugal that had now disappeared over the horizon, and the new land they had found last year.

He wasn't sure how long this trip would take. A lot depended on what they found south of the green land they had encountered last year and how heavy the ice floes were this year.

With one last look around his ship, Gaspar glanced at the grinning, weather-carved face of Fernam, his helmsman. There was no other man in his crew who seemed more at home on the sea. He had sailed on these voyages with Gaspar's father before and his knowledge of the stars allowed him to navigate these wild seas with impressive skill. It had taken little convincing to have him join his crew, and it gave Gaspar comfort to have him standing on the deck next to him. Although more than twice his age, Fernam showed him the respect he extended to Gaspar's father, believing a well-run ship needed a crew that respected their captain and followed his decisions without question.

With a smile, Gaspar nodded to Fernam and then made his way down the steps and through the heavy wooden door into his quarters, beneath the wheel deck.

4

The band was spread out behind him, every man, woman and child, trudging along the muddy footpath that wound through the trees alongside the quickly moving water of the nearby river. His eyes swept slowly along the long line of familiar faces that disappeared over the low ridge he had crossed a short time ago. He knew he would need to use all the fingers on his two hands more than three times to count them all, but he knew each of them by name. Like the ever-moving water of the nearby river, his people were also being drawn to the sea, just as they had been when the time of the snow was past for all the years of his life.

Days before this, the last of the snow had melted into the ground and the flow of the river had settled down again, receding to its normal size after the runoff found its way to the ocean. It was then their journey to the coast had begun, as it had every year.

Daygon tilted his head back and looked up at the blue sky that stretched as far as he could see. Here and there a wispy white cloud drifted lazily across the eternal blue that separated him from his ancestors. He drew in a deep breath through his nostrils, letting the scents fill his head. He loved this season with its promise of new life. The smells of the damp ground churned up by their passing, the rattling of the flowing river water tumbling over stones that unsuccessfully tried to block its path, and the lively chatter of the fluttering songbirds all heralded the soon arrival of the warm season. The time when all the extra clothing became an hinderance and could be shed like the thick coats of many of the forest animals.

After the long snow-time of inactivity, it was good to be outside doing something again. On a distant ridge on the other side of the river a herd of caribou was foraging for the new shoots only now finding their way through the awakening surface of the ground. Thick patches of shaggy fur hung from their flanks, not yet shed from their snow-season coats. Once the band reached the coast and set up camp, they would hunt these caribou and begin preparing for the next snow season. It was a never-ending cycle that he would be a part of until he grew old, and then his children would provide for the family. This was the way of the Beothuk since time began. It was a good way, he thought. A way that must be protected. It kept families together and made the band strong.

The gentle touch on his shoulder served to confirm what he already knew. He had felt her presence as she stepped up beside him. He turned his head and looked into Shandowee's lovely eyes, still amazed at the effect they had on him. It was the same churning inside as the first time she had looked his way seven warm seasons ago. Time had not been able to change that feeling, and he was happy it hadn't.

"What are you thinking my husband?" she said softly.

"I am thinking you are the loveliest woman in all the band," replied Daygon, with the trace of a smile beginning to crease his face.

"What puts you in such a fine mood?" she said with a laugh, as she slid her hand into his.

"It is the warm season, and tomorrow we will reach our old camp near the coast. You know I love to be near the sea. Is there any better sound than the waves rolling up on the stones of the beach to put you asleep? And of course, you asleep by my side," he added with a grin.

Reaching around her, he gently caressed the head of little sleeping Gadedoo, cradled in the thick folds of his mother's hood.

"He needs a little brother to keep him company," Daygon said with a smile.

"Perhaps a little sister," she replied with a twinkle in her eye.

"Perhaps."

"What are you doing, brother?" asked Bragadessh as he walked slowly by, dragging a hand slide laden with his family's possessions. "Shouldn't you be leading the band?" he asked, as he pulled the slide to the side of the path and stopped, allowing those following to pass.

"I'm admiring your beautiful family, little brother" Daygon replied with a grin.

The two boys and their older sister stopped behind the slide, dropped their sacks on the ground and crowded around Shandowee to try and see their sleeping baby cousin.

"Shh," whispered Shandowee, placing a finger against her lips, "he's sleeping."

Daygon looked at his brother's heavily laden slide. "Are you still sure you want to do this?" he asked.

"I am. Taddowish and I talked it over and we will not be returning to the snow camp. We will find another camp and stay at the coast this year."

"I would much rather you returned with us, but it is your decision to make, brother. You know I will think about you until the snow melts again."

"We will be fine. And we won't have to haul all the food for days, back up this trail to the winter camp. I'll be happy if I never have to do that again."

Daygon was about to reply when he was interrupted by shouting coming from the front of the line that had moved out of sight around the next bend in the trail.

He heard his name being called. It sounded as if there might be trouble. He began to jog toward the sound. Bragadessh had dropped the handles of the hand slide and ran alongside his brother. In his left hand he carried his aaduth (spear) that he had grabbed from the slide. He too sensed there might be trouble.

Rounding the bend, Daygon could see that the crowd had bunched up around Meroobish, one of the scouts he had sent out ahead of the band. Meroobish stood head and shoulders over everyone around him. He was the biggest man in the band and Daygon's fiercest fighter when the occasion required it.

As he reached the group and pushed through those at the back, Daygon could see blood on Meroobish's hands and chest.

"What happened? Are you hurt?" he asked, grabbing Meroobish by the arm.

"It is not my blood," Meroobish replied calmly in his deep rolling voice.

"Where are Assonwitt and Bashoodite?"

"Back there," Meroobish nodded with his head indicating the way he had come. "Assonwitt is dead and Bashoodite is badly injured. I came to get help for him."

"Who did this?" asked Bragadessh.

17

"The others. The Shannok (Mi'kmaq Indian)," Meroobish replied, spitting with distain on the ground.

A murmur of anger rippled through the group standing around them, accompanied by shaking of fists and spitting on the ground.

"How did this happen?" Daygon asked, gripping Meroobish by the upper arm.

"They surprised us. They were hiding by the side of the trail. I should have seen them, but I missed the signs. It should not have happened."

"How many were there?"

"Six. I killed one of them and cut another. He too may die."

"Where are they now?" asked Daygon, peering around Meroobish in the direction he had come.

"They ran into the woods. They are cowards. They are always cowards. They wouldn't stand and fight like real men because they are not."

Daygon looked at the men gathered around Meroobish. Selecting Meroobish, Bragadessh, Toorett, Modthamook, and Pugathoite, he said, "get your weapons and come with me. The rest of you stay and protect the band. We will go and find Bashoodite and then the Shannok. Keep everyone here until we return."

"I want to come with you," said Odusweet.

"No. It is not yet safe," said Daygon. "The Shannok may still be there."

"Bashoodite is my husband. He is hurt and needs my help," she argued.

"No," Daygon replied firmly. "You will stay here. If it is safe, I will send someone to get you." In his mind he remembered the ceremony he had performed to unite these two. It had been just before the snow season, just after the band had returned to the winter camp. Her belly was swollen with their first child now and Daygon understood her anguish upon hearing her husband was injured. It would not be wise to take her until they knew the Shannok had left, so she would have to wait a little longer until he was sure they were gone.

Odusweet was about to reply, but, feeling the hand of one of the women on her shoulder, bowed her head in submission and turned away as a tear slipped down her cheek and splashed on her extended belly.

She anxiously watched through blurry eyes as the six men ran down the path and disappeared. She lifted her head and whispered a prayer to the Great Spirit to keep her husband safe, while placing a hand on her large belly as if to reassure the unborn child.

Shandowee slipped her arm around Odusweet's waist and gently led her to the shade of a large birch tree and helped her sit with her back against its wide trunk. "You must get things ready for his return," she said. "He will need your help."

"What if his injury is too bad? What if it is too late to help him?" she sobbed. "What will we do then?"

"You must not think that way," Shandowee said. "You must be strong for him. That is what he would want."

5

Star trudged down the field pulling the heavy metal plow. Behind her Paublo struggled to keep the plow moving in a straight line. With the long reins looped over his head and around one shoulder he straddled the furrow being curled up by the iron plow as it bit into the rich soil, careful not to trip and get pulled by the big horse.

Mostly black, she sported a white shank on her left front leg, another white spot near the beginning of her tail, and a white mark on her forehead that resembled a star if you looked at it long enough. And so, the name stuck.

She never got excited about plowing the fields. It was hard work, and for what she wondered. If she got a chance to slow down or stop, she took it. Today Paublo was doing it for her. He kept stopping, leaning on the plow handles and gazing toward the harbour. He clearly had something else on his mind. That was fine by Star.

Paublo was having trouble getting Star moving again each time he stopped. He was having even more trouble keeping his mind on his work. After the second pass he had discovered that when he gazed at the distant beach he could actually see the fish stall. He realized he had been able to see it all along. She was there all the time and he hadn't even known it.

Work did not progress well that day. He spent too much time staring at the tiny stall, hoping to catch a glimpse of her. Several times he caught himself examining his hand where she had touched him. He had to find a way to get back to the beach.

When it finally reached stopping time, he had only finished half the field, which was about half as much as he should have done. Nevertheless, he could do no more with darkness approaching. He unhitched the plow and guided Star toward the barn. She needed little coaxing. She was done for the day as well.

Once Star was fed he headed for the house, his muscles aching and his belly growling. Before stepping up on the bridge he glanced over his shoulder at the harbour. Darkness had crept over its shores and there was nothing to see except in his imagination.

The cooking smell drifting out from the house made his mouth fill with saliva. He realized how hungry he was and ran up the steps and into the kitchen.

"Happy Birthday," his mother greeted him and threw her arms around his neck, holding him a little longer than usual.

"Wash up and come and sit, boy," said his father from his seat at the table.

Paublo expected a reprimand for not getting his work done, but surprisingly it never came. Perhaps later, he thought as his eyes scanned over the feast his mother had laid on the table.

He could not remember when dinner had tasted so good. He barely lifted his head from his plate. He knew the fish tasted better because it was the one Maria had picked. He would not forget this birthday. If only she could have been at the table. That would have made it perfect.

When he finally pushed his plate away and leaned back in his chair, he noticed both his mother and father were watching him, broad smiles on their faces.

"I have news, son," his father said.

Paublo noticed his mother's smile fade. He was not sure what was coming next. Was this bad news, he wondered? Inwardly he began to brace himself.

"I have your berth, Paublo."

"My berth?"

"With Captain Gaspar."

Paublo stared at his father in disbelief.

His father smiled and nodded.

Paublo leaped up, overturning his chair with a crash. He couldn't believe what he was hearing. This day could not be any better.

He rushed to his father and grabbed him in a bear hug. His father returned it in a rare show of affection.

This was the news he had dared to hope for. It also gave him the perfect excuse to go to the docks whenever he wasn't busy with chores. Life was suddenly very good.

"Captain Gaspar has sailed to Lisbon with his brother for supplies and will be returning in a few weeks. He will then be joined by Captain Antonyo in the third ship, the one that is tied up at the docks. You will join Captain Gaspar's crew then," his father said.

"Weeks. How will I be able to wait for weeks?"

"There's lots of work to be done."

Paublo noticed his mother wipe the corner of her eye with her apron just before she turned and busied herself with the dishes. He forced himself to look away. Although his insides were churning to see her like that, he wanted this more than anything and he hoped she would accept it in time.

6

He thought he was getting better at finding excuses to go to the beach. He was pleased with himself that no one had discovered his real reason. He always made sure to pass the fish stall on his way to the ship dock, but it wasn't until his third trip that he saw her again.

She waved to him as he was passing by. "Hey Paublo," she called.

His heart jumped. He felt it in his chest. "Hi Maria," he replied as he turned off the path to stand next to the stall.

"What brings you here today? Did you enjoy the fish?

Her voice was as musical as he remembered. "It was good, really good," he replied.

"Looking for another?"

"Not today. Today I'm watching for Captain Gaspar's ship to return from Lisbon."

"Why?" she asked, as she lifted a fish from the cart and placed it in a barrel.

"I'm joining his crew when he returns."

"They say he is going exploring again."

"He is, and I'm going too. Isn't that great."

"That's exciting Paublo. Imagine being the first to see new lands, the first to set foot on them."

The thought occurred to Paublo that he was talking to her and his breathing was normal, well almost.

The next few days passed by in a blur. He met Maria most every day and, as the week progressed, he began to wonder if he was making the right decision. Could he go that long without seeing her, without hearing her voice. His decision began to weigh on him more and more. It was what he had always wanted, and he would see her when he returned, he rationalized. He wished there was some way to take her voice with him.

The stolen kiss behind the stall, about a week later, almost destroyed his resolve, and if she hadn't encouraged him to take the trip with Captain Gaspar he would have cancelled it there and then. It seemed she was happy for his adventure. It was the promise of more kisses when he returned that would get him through the long days on the ocean.

It was probably fortunate for him that the ship appeared on the horizon the next day.

7

The night had passed quickly. Even though the anticipation and excitement of setting out into the unknown had kept sleep at bay for a short time after he'd stretched out on his bunk, the gentle rocking of the ship had lulled him to sleep, as it always did.

Now the creaking and groaning of the planks as the ship pushed its way through the sea was the most welcome sound he could have asked for. It was a sound he had missed while waiting for the long winter to pass.

Cook had just left his quarters, leaving behind a strong aroma of coffee. Few even knew his name was Nuno, thought Gaspar. He had been known as Cook for so long most had forgotten the name he'd been christened with. Gaspar wondered if the big man would even respond to Nuno anymore.

The first time Gaspar met Nuno was on the first voyage he took with his father, several years before. His ever-positive outlook on life accompanied with his unmatched skills in the galley made him a favorite of all the crew. Despite the overpowering presence of his six foot, three-hundred-pound frame, he was better known for the hearty laugh that filled any room he entered.

He could wield the large kitchen cleaver as if it were an extension of his hand, probably as well as any of the soldiers could handle their swords. Gaspar expected he could hold his own in a close fight if the cleaver was involved. It would not be pleasant being on the receiving end of it.

Gaspar had found himself smiling at the broad back as Cook ducked his head, stepped over the threshold, and closed the door softly behind him. He was glad he had been able to convince him to join the crew. He knew the voyage would be more enjoyable because of it.

On the thick polished planks of the tabletop, next to the steaming coffee, sat the charts his father had given him a short time before he had died. That was a mere five years ago, yet it seemed much longer. The loss had a left a gaping hole in their family which he knew he was expected to help fill. Maybe after this voyage, he thought. For now, it would be up to young Vasco to manage things.

He took a seat on the worn wooden stool and leaned over the chart. Some of the scribblings he had watched his father make on their last voyage together. Some were much older. Others were his own, made on last years voyage. In the bottom right corner was his father's name, Joao Vaz Corte-Real, inked with the familiar flair of his father's handwriting.

Gaspar hoped this year would prove more profitable than last year's voyage. The thick ice he had encountered had made it impossible to reach the land and he had been forced to turn back with little to show but an abundance of fish. It was not what King Manuel had expected, and he knew there would be no third voyage if things didn't go better this year.

Studying the chart, he determined to sail south this year once land became visible. He suspected there was land to the south and if there was, there probably would be natives for the taking. What else they would find remained to be seen. He took the steaming mug, lifted it to his mouth and tipped it up, savoring the pungent taste of the hot black liquid before swallowing.

King Manuel had made it clear he wanted Gaspar to claim the new lands he found for Portugal. He believed the land discovered by John Cabot in 1497 fell within the territory assigned to Portugal by the treaty with Spain. Before allowing him to leave the royal court, the king had reaffirmed his expectation to Gaspar to fly the flag of Portugal on that very land.

Gaspar's eyes fell on the written commission with King Manuel's royal seal now broken where the paper had been folded. He took another deep drink of the strong coffee as he slid the document to the corner of the chart and tucked it underneath the iron paperweight.

Turning in his stool, he reached out and pulled the ship's log from the shelf. Flipping the pages to yesterday's date, he dipped the quill in the open ink bottle and began to record that day's travel.

8

With Meroobish in the lead and Daygon following close behind the six of them broke into a run, following the path along the riverbank. The trail was still wet and muddy in places where the spring sun had not yet penetrated through the tangle of underbrush, making the going slippery. In those shady places more attention had to be taken with the path than the surrounding woods.   That worried Daygon. Although he didn't expect it, the Shannok might have doubled back. They had ambushed his men once and he didn't want that to happen again. He gripped his hathemay (bow) a little tighter, squeezing the notched arrow between his fingers as he ran behind the towering bulk of Meroobish.

He had followed Meroobish into battle before, and against the same enemy.   There was no other warrior he would rather have at his side. He was fearless and fought with a single-mindedness when the battle lust came upon him. Daygon knew he would rather be on his side than facing him. He thought he understood why the Shannok ran away.

The other four ran behind him, single file on the narrow path. They were all good men, men who would willingly put themselves in danger to protect the band. He knew they were running into battle and he wondered how this day would end.

It had been a while since there had been trouble with the Shannok and Daygon feared they had let their guard down. He wondered what had triggered this attack. They couldn't be trusted and he should have been more careful. They should not be allowed to hunt and fish here. This was Beothuk country, and it should stay that way. They would hunt these troublemakers down and make them pay for this. *We will make an example of them and it will serve as a warning to any more of them who might consider coming onto our land,* he thought, as he kept one eye on the woods and one on the path.

Ahead of him, Meroobish slowed. Daygon held up his hand to warn those behind him.

"We are here," said Meroobish, speaking over his shoulder in his deep rumbling voice, while continuing to scan the woods ahead of them.

Stepping around him, Daygon surveyed the scene, picturing the ambush in his mind. Just a few strides ahead, Assonwitt lay on his face at the side of the path with two arrows sticking out of his back. A short distance from him lay one of the Shannok, his head tilted at an odd angle, lifeless eyes staring up at the evening sky. Bashoodite was propped against the base of a large birch tree on the other side of the path, his head sagging onto his bloody chest. His long braid had fallen forward and hung over his face like a thick rope. His right hand was firmly closed around his aaduth that lay on the ground at his side. The left leg of his pants was soaked in blood where the broken shaft of a Shannok spear was sticking through the material that covered his thigh. He was not moving.

The bubbling water from the nearby river and the quickened breathing of his men were the only sounds that broke the stillness of this place of death.

"Check him," Daygon said to Bragadessh, nodding in the direction of Bashoodite. "Keep an eye on the woods," he said to the others, who stood with hathemays and aaduths at the ready, covering the trail behind them as well as in front.

Bragadessh walked to the still form of Bashoodite. He bent to one knee moved the braid aside and placed his hand lightly over Bashoodite's mouth. He looked back at Daygon and shook his head. "There is no breath in him. He is already gone, brother," he said, as he pushed to his feet.

Toorett walked to the Shannok, kicked his side and spat in his face. "We will find your friends," he hissed. "Then they will join you."

"Find their trail," Daygon said. "Let's hunt," he said, with anger rising in his voice.

9

Paublo sat astride the flat top of a tying post at the end of the dock, just as he had each day for the last three days. After finishing his work in the gardens, he had come here to eat his lunch and watch, and to smell the scents of the harbour. His father had been a farmer since Paublo was born, so the smells of the soil and the animals were all too familiar. He lived in it day and night, but he felt something different when he got to smell the sea. It seemed to cleanse him and to stir a longing to sail its expanse and discover its mysteries where it washed upon the shores of lands far from here.

Paublo shifted his seat on the post. He could barely contain his excitement. He knew the time was near. Captain Antonyo's ship had been outfitted and now sat at anchor, waiting for the arrival of Captain Gaspar's ships. Paublo had heard the men talking. They said the ship would arrive in a few days. Paublo did not want to miss the arrival. He knew he was of little use to his father these days. He could not keep his mind on the work, and when he was not down sitting on the dock his mind was.

He glanced up from watching the fish swimming lazily just beneath the surface around the posts at the head of the dock, and there it was. The sails of the ship were visible coming around the Great Rock. The flag at the top of the main mast was Captain Gaspar's. He could sit still no longer. He jumped to his feet and began to run back up the hill to where his father was feeding Star. Maria was not at her stall, so he kept running. He had to tell someone.

As he ran, his mind went back to how all this had happened.

When the news had first spread around the village that Gaspar was mounting another expedition in search of the new world, he began working on his father. He remembered the conversation that he believed may have finally convinced him.

"You can get me on that ship, father," he'd commented, as he stood at the back of the wagon scattering the manure with his shovel.

"What ship is that?" muttered his father, as he pulled the reins to turn the horse around for another pass down to the end of the field.

"Captain Gaspar's. You've heard about his new voyage."

"I've heard. Not much came of the one last year."

"They say he found land but couldn't get to shore because of thick ice."

"Heard that. Seems like a waste to go back there again, don't it?"

"He'll know where to go this time. Imagine what he might find. Wouldn't you want to be a part of that?"

"Never understood what you find interesting out there," he said, waving his hand toward the sea. "It's just water. Demands a lot more lives than the land does." He clicked his tongue and waved the reins to get more speed out of the plodding horse. Star just shook her head in annoyance and continued at the same pace.

"I don't know, father. There's something that's drawing me to it. It is like it is something I have to do."

"What makes you think I can get you a berth? You're only sixteen, and a small one at that. There're lots of men around who have been to sea before."

"They'll need a cabin boy. I'll do anything."

"Maybe he's already got a full crew from Lisbon. That is where he is headed to in a few weeks to outfit his ships."

Paublo remembered throwing another shovel full in a wide arc across the field behind them.

"They owe you, father. They said it themselves. You've told us many times how they said they would do anything for you after you found their father, confused and lost, after wandering out on the moor in the night the year before he died."

"They don't owe me nothing, son. That's not how life works."

"But they said it."

"Don't mean it is the way it gotta be."

"You could ask, father. You know the family. Please father?"

His father nodded and turned back to the horse. "Guess I could," he had mumbled. "Your mother won't be pleased though."

Paublo couldn't believe his ears. He hadn't stopped grinning the rest of that day.

10

Last night he had received a message from the ship to report to the dock first thing in the morning. Sleep had evaded him. Daybreak found him walking away from the house, his mother and father standing just outside the open door. He dared not look back for fear he would see his mother's tears.

Passing the empty fish seller's stall, his mind turned to Maria. He hoped she would await his return. She had said she would. She was probably already on the water with her father. They usually left before sunrise. He glanced out the harbour but could not see their boat. Maria had told him they always flew a blue banner from the top of the single mast of their little boat. There were boats, but nothing blue.

Paublo began to whistle and continued on to the dock where the ship was tied up. He stood there looking up at the deck of the ship, craning his head back to see all the way to the top of the tallest mast. He could barely contain his excitement as his eyes ran over all the ropes and sails attached, knowing he was going to spend time on this boat. He knew he had much to learn. He just wanted to get started.

Standing just a few feet from him on the dock was one of the black slaves from up at the big house. He had been deposited there by a wagon a short while before. The bag slung over his shoulder seemed to indicate he was going on the ship as well.

Paublo eyed him out of the corner of his eye. He was much older than him. His wooly hair had turned white and his face showed deep lines of age. He had never talked to a slave before, and he wondered if he should now.

They were the only two standing on the dock, so it appeared they were the only ones who would be boarding the ship once the gangplank was laid down.

He looked back up at the ship and watched several sailors scamper up the ropes and out onto the crossbeams where they began to remove the bindings of the sails. *They are surefooted,* he thought. *Wonder if I could do that.*

"What's your name?" he blurted, without taking his eyes from the action above.

The man was silent for a moment, then slowly turned his head. "Name's Bo," he said.

The gangplank rattled as a sailor swung it out and let it drop near their feet. He motioned for them to board.

"I'm Paublo," he said, as he grabbed the guide rope and hurried up the rickety plank.

When he reached the deck, he looked over his shoulder. The black man still stood there, his bare feet inches from the end of the plank.

He glanced up at the wheel deck where Captain Gaspar stood scowling down at the slave. "Get him up here," he snapped to the sailor. "It's time to get underway."

"Git on board," yelled the sailor, "Er I'll drag ya on."

Bo lifted his eyes and fixed them on Paublo, tentatively placed a foot on the swaying plank, then with a rush ran the rest of the way and dropped to his knees on the deck.

The watching crew showered him with taunts and jeers. Paublo turned and followed a sailor who was waving to him at the open door of the hatch.

11

Bo jumped from the wagon and lifted the small cloth bag from the back. Everything he owned was in that bag. He had been told yesterday that he was going on the ship with Master Gaspar. Last night he hadn't slept. He was both terrified and excited. He wasn't sure how he would be able to board the ship because the memories of that horrible trip here in the bottom of a ship were still strong, but it might be his chance to get back home. He knew he really had no choice anyway. If they said he was going on the ship, then he was going.

He looked at the back of the boy standing near the edge of the dock in front of the ship. He looked small to be boarding the ship. He had a bag slung over his shoulder as well. The bag looked fuller than his.

He stood near the boy and waited. The ship looked enormous from here. He was frightened. He did not want to leave the land. It looked like the ship was moving all the time, rising and falling against the dock. His brow began to sweat. Maybe to escape this way was not a good idea. He felt his eyelids were twitching rapidly, and he closed and open his eyes firmly, trying to make it stop. He wished he were back at the big house.

"What's your name?" came from the boy standing next to him.

What's he talking to me for? wondered Bo.

Finally, he said, "Name's Bo."

A large plank was swung out and the end dropped to the dock with a crash near their feet. Bo jumped nervously.

He watched as the boy eagerly hurried up the swaying bridge. He heard him say over his shoulder, "My name is Paublo."

He couldn't get his feet to move. He was frozen with fear. Above him he heard a sailor yelling at him. He forced his eyes upward and looked directly into the boy's. He lifted his foot and ran, collapsing in a heap on the deck. He heard the jeers and laughing.

The plank was hauled aboard and lashed to the rail.

He became aware of the movement of the ship. He thought he might be sick.

He felt a huge hand close around his arm and lift him to his feet. "I'm Cook," the giant said, "You're coming with me."

The man called Cook held his arm in a firm grip and led him toward a big hatch. The closer they got the more afraid Bo became. He did not want to go down into that hole. All of the terrors of the ship that brought him from his home lurked down there in the dark. He pulled back against the giant's grip, but the giant didn't even seem to notice.

When they reached the stairs, Cook pushed him down ahead. Bo could still hear the shouts and jeers of the crew who were watching.

At the bottom, Cook gripped his arm again and led him to the galley. Bo lifted his eyes and looked around. The small room was well lit with lanterns hanging from the walls. Pots and large metal stirring spoons hung from the low ceiling, occasionally clanging together with the motion of the ship. The smell of cooking food filled the room.

"You will work for me down here," said Cook, handing him a food-stained piece of sail cloth that served as an apron. "You don't have to go down any further if you don't want. The food is stored on this deck. Nothin' below only the crew quarters. 'Spect you don't want to be down there, by the sound of them up on deck."

"No sir," Bo nodded.

"You will take the captain's food to him when I can't and bring back his dirty dishes when he's done with 'em. You will peel the vegetables and help me cook and then clean up the tables after the crew eat. You done any cookin?"

"Some."

"Guess we'll get along fine then."

"Yes sir."

"Now let's get to work on dinner."

12

"Over here," shouted Toorett, at the edge of the small clearing, where he was down on one knee. "They left this way," he said pointing toward the path leading to the coast.

The others hurried to where he was bent over the footprints in the churned-up mud. "They must have returned and gathered here after Meroobish left to get help," said Toorett.

"They probably finished off Bashoodite when they returned," said Meroobish. "He was alive when I left. The cowards must have hidden in the woods and waited for me to go."

"This path will lead them to the coast," said Modthamook.

"They probably have a boat there," said Toorett.

"We must hurry. They must not get away," said Bragadessh.

"They have a half day start on us. Will we be able to catch them now?" asked Pugathoite. "Perhaps it is already too late."

"Look there. See, it is blood on the leaves. One of them is bleeding just as Meroobish said."

"Let's hope it slows them down."

"It will."

They all turned and looked at Daygon, waiting for his decision.

"We can not let them escape," said Daygon, looking at each of his men. "They must pay for what they did here." Each of them nodded in turn. Their eyes reflected the battle lust he felt in his own heart.

"Let's go get them," he said, and broke into a run with the others following close behind.

13

Paublo followed the sailor down the stairs, past the galley and then down a second set of stairs to the lower deck. The windowless room they entered was dimly lit by candlelight. A row of hammocks was strung on each side, providing a narrow aisle down the middle. The air was heavy with the smell of tar and candle smoke mingled with the scent of unwashed bodies. At the very back of the long room, in the far corner, was his hammock. As he dropped his bag in the tiny space underneath it, he wondered where Bo would be sleeping. He'd heard the jeers as he was descending the stairs. He didn't expect he'd be sleeping down here with the crew.

"Leave your stuff here," said the sailor. "My name's Francisco. Been on a boat before?"

"This is my first time."

"What I thought. That bucket there is for getting sick in. Keep it under your hammock. You're going to need it. 'Tis your responsibility to keep it clean. Nobody else will be doing it for you. Now follow me topsides. You got a lot to learn, boy."

Following Francisco past the galley, he heard voices inside. One was unmistakable in its rich tone as that of the black slave.

He put his hand to the door frame to see inside when Francisco said, "Come on boy. There's nothing in there for you. Get a move on now. Up the stairs with ya."

As they emerged from the hatch into the early morning sunshine, the deck was full of sailors engaging in the many jobs needed to get the ship underway. It seemed everyone knew where they were supposed to be and what they were supposed to be doing. Paublo stood next to Francisco watching it happen, excitement coursing through him as the lines were cast away from the dock and the ship began to move out through the harbour under partial sail. He looked up at the top of the tallest mast. Captain Gaspar's flag fluttered there in the light breeze.

He glanced back at the hillside where a lone figure stood next to a horse and wagon, a straw hat held up to shield his eyes from the glare of the sun as he watched the ship draw away.

For a moment a sadness washed over him, quickly replaced with excitement as he realized he had made it. He was finally going to sea.

"One of your responsibilities is to clean the Captain's Quarters every day after he leaves it in the morning," said Francisco. "Make sure you get in there as soon as he is out. Don't ever let him come back to a dirty room. Don't mess with anything on the tables. Leave the charts and logbooks alone. Open the window if it is a good day, to air the place out. You got all that?"

"I do. What's it like up there?

"Where?"

"Up there at the top of the mast."

"Don't know. Can't go up there. Ain't got the stomach for it."

"When do I get to try?"

"Why would you want to try that?"

"I want to learn every part of the ship. Beside it must have the best view on the ship."

More sailors walked out across the long crossbeams, released the remaining sails which immediately filled with wind and snapped tight, straining the ropes anchored to the deck.

Paublo felt the ship respond as it tilted a little to one side and began to pick up speed, hungrily biting into the waves. Looking back over the stern, he spotted the little blue banner fluttering from the mast of a little fishing boat. His heart leaped. It was Maria. He waved to the tiny figure standing at the bow. He thought she waved back but he couldn't be sure. He hoped so.

The other two ships followed directly in their wake as they cleared the harbour. The voyage was underway. Nothing but promise lay out there on the horizon.

14

The midday African sun beat down on the tiny village, scorching the ground, forcing the inhabitants under any available shade. The warm breeze from the nearby river provided little relief from the sun's searing rays. At this time of the day only the children ventured beyond the thatched huts. He idly watched them through the door opening as they splashed in the lazily flowing water. The wavy heat distorted his vision so that at times the children were just formless shadows, like something from one of his dreams. Tired from squinting against the bright sun, his eyes slowly closed, and he surrendered to sleep.

It was the silence that alerted him and nudged him awake again. The children's shouts of joy had stopped. He shook his head and blinked the sleep away. The children were all standing in a group in the shallow water, staring toward the clearing as if something had scared them. With apprehension and the beginnings of alarm, he pushed his head through the opening of the grass hut to be met by his worst nightmare. The clearing was surrounded by white men in their wide brimmed hats and their black traitor guides, all of them carrying guns, or machetes. He knew what this meant. He had heard stories from other villages where these traders had raided and taken away all the men. No one had any idea where those captured went but they never returned, so the stories went.

He tried to duck back into the safety of the hut, but he had been spotted. Rough hands grabbed his arms, pulled him through the door and threw him to the ground at the center of the clearing. Rope was tied around his hands and then to the other men of the village. Women were crying and gathering the children, pushing them into the huts where they hoped they would be safe.

He knew that if the stories were true there was no escape, and he suspected they were. He stayed on his knees, his head bowed in submission. He hoped his grandson would not return to the village before this was over. He did not want him to be taken. He could not bear that.

This was the recurring nightmare that left Bo in a cold sweat and rendered him sleepless. It was still dark, the night still had far to go. He pulled the tattered blanket tighter around his neck and tried to push the thoughts away. He realized this was not only a dream but his reliving the memories of that day when he was taken from his home. It was not only on his mind when he was awake but now haunted his dreams as well. He hoped this ship was taking him back there. He dozed again.

15

The day had been a full one once they had cleared the harbour and set sail for the new land. He had tried to watch everything the sailors did, to understand what all the ropes were for and how they were to be adjusted on their pulleys to allow the sails to capture the most wind. He liked feeling the impact in his legs as the ship dropped from one wave to the next. He tasted, for the first time, the salt in the spray that was flung back over the ship. He had followed Francisco around the deck as he pointed out the various parts of the ship, listening intently, not wanting to miss a thing he said.

He noticed Francisco walked with a limp that became more obvious the more he walked.

"What happened to your leg," he asked, as they leaned against the rail at the very front of the ship.

"Broke it," muttered Francisco.

"How?"

"Fell, I did. From up there," he said pointing upward. "Lucky I didn't kill myself. Broke my leg in two places, is all. Won't catch me up there again."

"I'd like to try it."

"Maybe tomorrow, but it won't be me showing you how. Time for supper now."

Paublo took one last look around and followed Francisco below. He found a seat and ate ravenously what was ladled onto his plate by Bo.

Later, lying in his hammock, he could not find sleep, although the light snoring in the darkness around him and the gentle swinging motion should have made it easy. His mind was racing with all he had seen and the excitement and promise of new things tomorrow.

He swung down to the floor, pulled on his trousers and slipped his tunic over his head. Carrying his boots in one hand, he felt his way through the maze of hammocks and stepped outside the door into the hallway. The air was easier to breathe out here. Stepping into his boots he climbed the steps to the hatchway and onto the deck. Overhead the dark sky was studded with twinkling lights, surrounding the full silver moon. The light wind on his face carried the salty scent of the sea. He drew it deep into his nostrils. The night was filled with the creaking and groaning of the ship as it pushed through the sea.

Rounding the side of the raised hatch, he almost walked into the sleeping form stretched underneath a blanket. The moonlight shone off the white wooly cap crowning Bo's head.

Although he thought he hadn't made a sound, the figure stirred.

"What you want?" Bo asked.

"Nothing," replied Paublo. "I couldn't sleep."

"You'd best do that. They'll start your work tomorrow."

"Why are you sleeping here?" asked Paublo as he took a seat on the deck with his back propped against the hatch wall.

"Can't sleep down there. Too many nightmares."

"Nightmares?"

"Yes."

"Why?"

"That's how I was brought to Portugal. Chained up down there, different ship but still the same."

Paublo was quiet for a few minutes and then said, "Must have been terrible."

"It was. They took most of the men from our village. Some of them died down there."

"Where are the rest?"

"Took them to Lisbon. I was the only one who stayed on Terceira."

"Leave any family behind?"

"Yes."

"Sad."

"I will see them again. This ship will take me back."

Not wanting to upset Bo, Paublo decided not to tell him they were not sailing to Africa. It would only make things worse for him.

Pushing to his feet, he walked back to the hatch door and went back down the stairs to work some more on his sleep.

16

Bo pushed back the thin blanket. It was not yet light. Overhead the twinkling lights of his ancestors watched over him. He hoped someday they would bring him home, perhaps at the end of this voyage. He believed this was why he was on this ship. Each day would bring him closer to his home. He wondered which of the twinkling lights was his brother.

Far out on the horizon, the first glimmer of light from the approaching day appeared as a thin line. It would soon grow and cover the whole sky and the lights would disappear until darkness found them again. He knew it was time to get below before Cook came looking for him. That would mean punishment. He did not want that. He did not want any trouble now he was this close to getting back home.

He had slept well after the boy had left. The boy was different from the rest of the men on this ship. Most of them treated him like they would treat some animal. Some of them treated him as if he wasn't even there. The boy had shown him kindness. Maybe he was too young to know differently. Maybe he was just different and had kindness in his heart. Time would tell. At any rate he was the only friend he had on this ship. Maybe he would help him escape when the time came.

He pushed to his feet, folded the blanket, tucked it under his arm and made his way down the stairs to the galley.

Cook was beginning his work in the flickering candlelight. He was on his knees in front of the big stove shoving wood into the firebox.

"Fill those pots with water," he instructed, without looking up from the fire he was fanning into life.

Soon the little galley was filled with heat and the sounds of bubbling water and clanging pots signaled the approach of breakfast for the day crew.

"Take this to the Captain," ordered Cook, as he handed a tin tray with hot coffee and warm rolls to Bo.

"Yes sir."

"And hurry back. The men will be here in a few minutes. I will need you to serve them."

"Yes sir," said Bo, as he ducked his head and hurried up the stairs.

17

A soft rap on the door behind him brought Gaspar's mind back from the logbook lying open on the table in front of him. He had almost completed yesterday's entry of what had been another uneventful day. It had been a quick turnaround at the Terceira harbour. He hadn't even left the ship. He could have met Antonyo's ship outside if he hadn't had to pick up Bo and young Paublo. He was anxious to reach the land that needed exploring.

"Yes?" said Gaspar.

"Its me Cap'n sir," came from the other side of the door.

The unmistakable resonance of the African voice confirmed it was Bo.

"Come on in, Bo," said Gasper as he turned toward the door.

"Cook sent me with your breakfast, sir," said the tall, thin black man as he bent and stepped inside the quarters, his short, curly white hair a sharp contrast to the rich black tone of the skin on his bare chest. The food-stained britches he wore did not reach below his knees, and his bare feet made no sound on the wooden planks of the floor as he moved.

This was the first voyage Gasper had included Bo on, and other than the ship on which he had been brought to The Azores from the shores of the dark continent this would be only the second time he had sailed the oceans. Since he had arrived more than five years ago, he had been a servant in the Corte-Real household and had served the family well.

Gaspar knew Bo's first voyage had been spent in the hold of the ship in less than ideal conditions and hadn't been surprised when he'd been told Bo had slept outside on the deck of the ship last night. Cook had also told him it had taken some coaxing to get Bo below deck to help in the galley.

"How are you, Bo?" asked Gasper.

"Fine, sir," Bo replied, keeping his eyes on the floor.

"Has the sea made you sick?"

"No sir. Been good, sir."

"Good. Perhaps this is where you belong."

"Perhaps, sir."

"Has Cook been treating you well?"

"Yes sir."

Gasper picked the mug from the tray and lifted it to his lips, savoring the taste and sensation of the hot liquid flowing down his throat.

Bo placed the tray on the desk and padded noiselessly across the wooden floor in his bare feet. No one had been able to convince him of the necessity of wearing boots. He continued doing what he was most comfortable with, what he'd done all his life.

As he turned to pull the door closed, his eyes met Gaspar's for a brief moment before he averted them and bowed his head in subservience.

Gasper sat there staring at the closed door in thought. There was something in those dark eyes that troubled him, something that he suspected was being supressed. He wondered if he should keep a closer watch on him.

His family had always treated Bo well since his father had selected him from a shipment of captives that arrived on a ship from the African coast.

His sister, Jo, had called him Bo when she first saw him, and the name had stuck.

Gaspar sometimes wondered what family Bo had left on those dark shores. It looked as if Bo might be older than him, so he most likely did leave someone behind. He was glad he was fortunate enough to have been born into a family that had slaves rather than having to endure a lifetime of slavery like

Bo. Unfortunately for Bo, that was his lot in life, and if the look Gaspar had seen in his eyes meant Bo was thinking otherwise, he would have to make sure he understood his place. He glanced at the drawer where he had stored the coiled whip. He had brought it for use with the new slaves he hoped to capture in the new land. He hoped it wouldn't be necessary to use it on Bo.

18

Bo closed the cabin door and stood upright again. He too had glanced at the drawer where the whip was stored. He knew it was there because he had been alone in the cabin yesterday before the captain had retired for the night. The drawer had been left partially open at the time so he could not help seeing it. He hated that whip. The memory of it biting into his bare back remained fresh even though it was more than four years ago now.

He hated the white men who captured him and tore him from his family. He hated even more the black men who helped them, but they were far away, and he could do nothing about that. Maybe the white men he could do something about, someday. He would wait and watch.

He clung to the memory of his younger brother's dying cries as he lay in the darkness of the hold of the boat sailing to Captain Gaspar's land. The chains he had fought to try and reach his brother had left him bleeding, the raised scars on his wrists a constant reminder of that horrifying trip. Someday someone would pay.

He remembered the day they were all herded onto the rolling deck, chained together like animals. The white sailors had doused them with buckets of cold seawater to wash the filth from their bodies. It had been refreshing to breathe the fresh air again and the seawater had been welcome, despite the pain it caused on the open cuts on his wrists and ankles. The relief had been short-lived as his attention was drawn to several of the sailors dragging bodies up the hatchway stairs. He watched as one of them gripped his brother's lifeless body by the heels and dragged him across the deck to the rail. He tried to move toward him, but the chains restrained him. He had watched helplessly as they tossed his brother overboard along with several others dead or dying, for he was sure some of them still had some life in them. Those memories still haunted his dreams and fueled his hatred for these people.

He hated Captain Gaspar and his family for enslaving him. He pretended not too, but behind the mask he was watching for his chance to escape. He knew it would come someday.

He was pleased when Captain Gaspar decided to take him on the ship. Even though it was frightening to go below deck, he thought the ship might take him back to his homeland. That was when he would make his escape. If he had to kill Captain Gaspar to do that, he would have no regrets.

The only one he might spare would be young Paublo, and he wasn't sure about that yet. He was the only white man on this ship who had spoken to him as if he were a man.

He averted his eyes and bowed his head as he passed three of the sailors before stepping on the ladder of the hatch that would take him below to the galley. They all think they are safe, he thought, with an inward smile. I will wait until this ship takes me to my homeland. Then they will see who is safe.

The smell of cooking meat met him at the door of the galley. Cook looked up as he bent and entered.

"Where have you been?" he said gruffly. "I need help here."

"Getting the captain's dishes like you told me, sir," he replied.

"What took you so long?"

"Don't know, sir."

"Get those vegetables peeled and cooking. 'Twill soon be mealtime."

"Yes sir." *Perhaps Cook will be the first to go,* he thought.

19

It was the first full day out of Terceira. The sun had cleared the horizon and begun its climb into the largely cloudless sky. Standing on the bridge, Gaspar watched the day begin.

Below deck, Paublo was being pulled from a wonderful dream that featured Maria by Francisco, who was vigorously shaking his shoulder. "Get up, boy," he said, just inches from his face. "No sleeping in here. There's work to be done."

Paublo shook his head groggily. It felt like he had just closed his eyes, and he resented not seeing the end of the dream. The strength of Francisco's morning breath cleared the cobwebs in his head, and he turned his head away as he pushed from his hammock.

Hastily pulling on his boots and outer clothes, he hurried after Francisco as he stepped through the door into the crowded hallway. They followed the day shift up the stairs to the galley.

Paublo selected one of the bowls of hot oatmeal that Bo was spooning up and followed Francisco to one of the tables. Bo did not meet his eyes.

"Hey boy. So, you want to climb the ropes, do ya?" said a bearded sailor directly across the table, with a taunting laugh.

Lifting his eyes from the steaming cereal, Paublo noticed the other men around the table were watching him, most of them with grins on their faces.

Seeing the challenge in their eyes, Paublo nodded to the sailor but did not reply. He returned his eyes to the bowl.

"What make you think you can climb up there, boy," needled the sailor. "Men a lot older and stronger than you won't venture up there. Look at old Francisco there. We can't get him any higher than the top deck. He going to show you how?"

The table erupted in laughter.

"Bet I can climb faster than any of you, " Paublo blurted without stopping to think, immediately wishing he could get it back.

"Oh, do ya now?"

Conversation stopped at the two other tables. Paublo felt every eye in the room on him. He glanced toward the galley wicket. Bo's dark eyes watched him. He nodded slightly and turned back to his serving pot.

"I do," he said, with a confidence he didn't feel.

Looking around, the embolden sailor announced, "Here's what I think. If he loses, he has to stay up there and take two shifts on lookout."

"And what if he wins," someone laughed.

"Don't have to worry about that. Can't happen."

Laughter rippled around the room.

Sailors began pounding the table in anticipation of some good sport to break the monotony of the day.

"Finish your meal. You'll need it," said Francisco out of the corner of his mouth. "Gits mighty cold up there too. Especially later in the day."

Paublo scraped the remaining meal from the bowl and pushed back from the table as he swallowed it. *That was stupid*, he thought. He hadn't even set foot on those ropes before and he was going to race a sailor who did this for a living. He could only hope his opponent was one of the older ones. Of course, he knew he had lost when he opened his mouth.

Most of the sailors went up the stairs ahead of him and were standing on the deck watching as he emerged from the hatchway.

He glanced nervously around and with a sinking feeling saw the anticipation in their eyes. He noticed Captain Gaspar was also watching from the wheel deck. He tilted his head back and looked up to the top of the mast where the ship's colors fluttered in the wind. It was a long way up. This didn't feel like such a good idea anymore.

Francisco led him to the pulleys attached to the deck at the port rail. The sailor standing on the starboard side had broad shoulders and thick arms. Paublo noticed he had short legs, and he hoped it might somehow give him the advantage. It was the only thing he could see that might help him.

The crew began to chant, "Jorge, Jorge."

No one chanted his name.

Paublo was sure they had all seen this before. He wondered who the last victim was.

Jorge swung out on the ropes with his feet on the rail and looked across the deck with a grin, waiting for Paublo to do the same.

"Let's go boy," he shouted.

Paublo gripped the rope and pulled himself up. The thick fibers were rough and felt wet to his hand. He placed his feet on the ropes. They felt comfortable.

The chant for Jorge grew louder.

Jorge met his eyes and nodded.

Paublo began to climb, tentatively at first, but faster as they neared the first yardarm. He glanced across at the sailor. He was a step or two ahead of him. He was going to beat Jorge. Reaching his foot to gain the next step, he slipped. His foot came free and his body swung out with the motion of the sea, pulling his left hand off the rope. He was dangling by his right hand only, with his back to the ropes. His arm burned with the strain, then the ship rolled into the next wave, spinning him back to face the ropes. He looped his arm through and breathed again. Looking up he watched as Jorge reached the top and sat with his arm around the mast. He gathered his breath and continued climbing until he could reach Jorge's outstretched hand. Jorge's grip was firm and secure.

"Gave me a scare there for a minute," Jorge said. "Thought we might lose you. 'Tis a long way down."

Paublo nodded. His racing heart was returning to normal.

"Nothin' to break your fall if you slip," said Jorge.

Paublo looked down at the upturned faces far below. They looked so small, he thought curiously. Then he lifted his eyes to the two ships following in their wake. Everything was different up here. You could see so much further.

"Somethin' isn't it," said Jorge. "Never get tired of the view. Best place on the ship."

Paublo nodded, a half smile breaking across his face.

71

"Well, I best be getting down. You did well boy but you lost the bet, so you'll be up here a while."

"What about the Captain's quarters? I have to clean them."

"I'll have Francisco cover for you. Tie yourself on good. Don't want a fall. I'll have the black bring up your coat and hat. Gets cold later in the day."

Paublo watched as Jorge made his way back down to the deck. *This is my place,* he thought excitedly, as he wound the short length of rope that was tied to the mast around his waist.

Other than the two ships, there was nothing to see except water on all sides. With the rope securing him to the mast, he felt more confident and pushed himself to his feet on the yardarm, looping his arm around the mast for security. There was no sound other than the wind and the fluttering banner over his head. Far below the sailors had gone back to their work, the fun was over. He had lost the challenge just as everyone had expected, but for him it was a win. He had never dreamed he would be up here when he had wanted to go to sea, but this was where he wanted to be.

20

As Gaspar watched the boy climb it reminded him of his first voyage and how it felt to reach the top of the mast, and how small the sailors on the deck below had looked. This was the boy's initiation. Everyone knew he couldn't win the contest. It was something most sailors had to do on their first voyage. At sixteen, Paublo was the youngest on the ship, and by far the smallest. Gaspar had been reluctant to take him. His father had come to the house and petitioned Gaspar on behalf of his son. Eventually Gaspar agreed, out of respect for what Paublo's father had done for his own father the night he had wandered away.

Fernam, his helmsman, had been watching Paublo's progress as well. "Reminding you of your first time, Captain?" he asked, with a grin.

"It does, Fernam. I remember the freezing cold mostly, and the long hours clinging to the mast."

"We all had to do it," Fernam replied.

"Sort of a rite of passage, I guess," said Gaspar.

"I was thinking, Captain, what if we fasten one of them food barrels to the mast up there. He's small enough to fit in one and it would give him some protection against the wind and cold."

Gaspar looked at him thoughtfully. "Might work," he said. "He is small for his age. Think it can be made secure? There's a lot of motion up there."

"I think so. If anyone can make it secure it is Jorge. He's our best carpenter."

Gaspar nodded and called Jorge to the bridge after he had descended the ropes. Once he explained what he had in mind, Jorge peered up at the mast and nodded enthusiastically. "That's a great idea Cap'tn," he said. "Might have to take some sail off 'er while we work, but it can be done."

"OK then, lets do it," he ordered.

Jorge turned, hopped down the steps and headed for the hatch, calling two of the sailors to accompany him.

Gaspar called to Bo who was standing at the rail watching. "Take him up some food and warm clothes," he ordered.

Bo nodded and went below.

A short time later he emerged from the hatch and swung out onto the ropes. He climbed with confidence and sure feet as if he had done it all his life. He seemed to have no fear of heights like the boy. *The initial fear of the gangplank must have been the anxiety of getting on the boat in the first place,* thought Gaspar. *He seems to be alright now.*

Paublo watched Bo climb toward him.

"I lost the bet, Bo," he said, when the old man reached the yardarm.

"You were supposed to," said Bo, as he handed Paublo the bag of food and clothes."

"I suppose."

"Jorge has been doing this for his whole life. There was no way he could lose."

"Don't know why I said it. Just came out, without thinking."

"You will be the first to see land up here. I hope it is my land."

"I hope it is too, Bo."

"You'll need to put those clothes on. Capt'n says it will get cold up here."

"Thanks Bo."

Bo nodded and began the climb back down to the deck.

Paublo found a piece of bread in the bag and began to munch on it as he surveyed the empty sea in front of the ship. *Wish*

Maria could see me now, he thought. *Even better, I wish she could see the view from up here.*

21

The sun, often hidden by the grey clouds scuttling across its face, had climbed until it was directly overhead, when several sailors scaled the ropes and released the lower sails. Paublo watched them, wondering what was happening. The other two ships came within hailing distance and dropped sails as well. Captain Miguel's ship on the port side and Captain Antonyo's on the starboard. The ship, no longer in full sail, had slowed and was little more than drifting on the quiet seas.

On the deck below, Paublo saw two sailors emerge from the hatch carrying one of the food barrels, followed by Jorge who had a leather bag of tools hung around his neck and a wooden ledge he had crafted tucked under his arm. One of the sailors tied a coil of rope to Jorge's waist and he swung up to the ropes and started to climb upwards to where Paublo sat astride the yardarm, curiously watching him approach.

"What are you up to Jorge?" he asked, as the carpenter swung out onto the yardarm on the opposite side of the mast.

"We're going to make you a little more comfortable, son," said Jorge with a grin. "See that barrel down there? You and I are going to lash it to the mast once we get this ledge in place. That's going to be your home while you are up here. Now hold this in place against the mast while I drive those spikes home."

Paublo held the planks while Jorge hammered the long spikes through them, fastening into the mast. Then he wound a thin rope around the planks and tied it off. "That should make it secure enough," he said. "Now help me haul that barrel up. We are going to fasten it atop this shelf to make your new lookout. You should be small enough to fit inside it.

None of the other ships have one of these," he added.

"Will that be secure?"

"When I'm finished the mast would come down before the barrel does. It'll be a lot warmer in there and you won't have to hang on to the mast all the time. It'll be just like standing on the deck. Only difference is you will be able to see a lot further," he said with a smile.

Bracing against the swinging motion of the mast, Paublo began to pull on the rope with Jorge.

....

Standing next to the open hatch, Bo watched the activity high atop the mast. He wondered why they were hauling the barrel up there. *Perhaps it is a way to keep the boy up there for losing the bet,* he thought.

Most of the men around the ship were watching as well, including Captain Gaspar on the wheel deck.

Bo sniffed the air expectantly. He licked the salt from his lips. There was a storm coming. The taste was being carried by the wind.

He stared up again. The one called Jorge was fastening the barrel to the mast. *It must be for the boy to stand in,* reasoned Bo. *At least it should keep him from falling.*

A few minutes later his suspicions were confirmed when the boy climbed into the barrel, and Jorge began to descend to the deck.

Bo turned and went down the stairs to the galley.

22

The telltale prints of smooth, leather-shod feet carelessly left in the soft muddy patches of the trail showed how the Shannok felt about their enemy, the Beothuk. They knew they had frightened them away and wouldn't be followed. The Beothuk seldom took that chance. And if they did, more of them would die and that would be good. Then they could fish and hunt wherever they liked and not have to worry about them.

That was the story Daygon read in the footprints. He took the lead and set a fast pace. He knew they had a lot of ground to make up, and he hoped they caught their enemy before darkness fell. He slowed a little as he rounded another bend in the path, not wanting to run into an ambush, even though he didn't expect one. Just ahead, in a small clearing, he could see where the Shannok had stopped to eat. There was no sign of them, but the ashes of their fire were still warm when he pushed his hand into them. He pushed back the hair that had fallen across his face, looked up and smiled grimly at his brother.

"This was a mistake," said Bragadessh triumphantly. "They lost a lot of time here."

Daygon nodded. "They're not being careful. They have no idea we are following them," he said.

Modthamook bent and picked something up from the ground and held it up. It was a piece of discarded cloth that was caked in dried blood.

Turning to Meroobish, Daygon asked, "Where did you cut him?"

"His leg," Meroobish replied. "Right here," he said, indicating the outside of his upper thigh.

"Good. That will slow them as well. Looks like he is bleeding. They must have changed the cloth here."

"We are still far from the coast," said Bragadessh, glancing up at the graying sky. "It will be dark soon. They will camp for the night, I think."

"I think you are right, brother. They won't want to travel in the dark with the injured man, and they aren't worried about being followed."

"We will need to be more careful now," said Bragadessh quietly.

"No more talking. They may be close."

23

The deck shuddered beneath his feet as the ship dropped down from the crest of another wave and sliced into the next, sending a cascade of frothy water over the lower deck. The ropes and wet canvas creaked and groaned overhead, straining against the wind that fought to tear them free. Yesterday's calm sea was in a turmoil today. In the distance he could see the dark line of the approaching rain as the summer storm raced across the swirling water toward them.

Four of his men were climbing the ropes to trim the sails in preparation for the oncoming gale. High atop the mast he could just see young Paublo's head and shoulders above the edge of the barrel as the mast was swung in wide circles following the weaving of the ship as she charged her way through the angry sea.

Gaspar wondered if he should leave him up there. This was his first sea voyage. He hoped he had lashed himself to the mast like he'd been told, because this was only going to get worse.

He grabbed a rope as the bow of the ship reared upward, pushed by a wave larger than the last one. Struggling to stay on his feet, he glanced at Fernam, his helmsman, who was tying the rope attached to the base of the tall wheel around his waist.

"He'll be alright, Captain," he shouted above the roar of the wind. "The barrel will protect him."

"He's only sixteen. I'm not so sure," Gaspar replied, swaying with the motion of the deck. "He's never been in a storm like this."

"This'll test him for sure, but it's what he wanted," Fernam grunted, pulling the spokes of the wheel to counter the wave.

He was about to reply when out of the corner of his eye he saw one of the small row boats break its binding rope and tumble across the lower deck, rolling over one of the sailors in its path.

"Get that boat and lash it down," he roared, his voice lost in the wind.

Three sailors scrambled across the canting deck and grabbed onto the small boat, a fourth crawled to where the downed man lay on the deck pressed up to the rail, his head rolling with each pitch of the ship.

The ship reared back to climb the next wave and then violently slammed down into the trough, tossing the boat and sailors across the deck into the forward mast. The impact stove in the side of the boat, one of the splintered planks impaling Jorge against the mast. The other two managed to get ropes over the larger piece of the wreckage and lash it to the deck where it was. The rest was flung across the deck and disappeared over the side.

With the help of other sailors, they dragged Jorge across the sea-washed, heaving deck to the hatch and carried him below.

Gaspar looked to where the downed man had been pressed against the rail. Only his would-be rescuer was there, on his knees, clinging to the rope that tied him to the deck. He looked up at Gaspar and shook his head.

"Damn," roared Gaspar in frustration, slamming his fist against the rail. "That's two of my men down and we've only just started this voyage."

The dark wall of rain swept across the deck in horizontal sheets, making it impossible to see the whole length of the ship.

24

Paublo watched the dark line of clouds on the horizon. They seemed to be rushing toward the ship. Underneath the clouds the sea had turned white, whipped up by wind that had not yet reached them. The air had quickly grown colder. He cupped his hands and blew into them. Sharp flashes of light laced the approaching clouds. It was a storm. It looked like a big one and it was coming fast. The ship was already battling through larger waves. The motion at the top of the mast was getting much more violent. He checked his safety rope and pulled on his woolen mitts. Even though the barrel was a tight fit he was being thrown around with the lurching of the ship. Without it he would not have been able to stay at the top of the mast.

Below, on the deck, sailors were lashing down anything that could move. On the wheel deck he could see the tiny figures of the captain standing next to Fernam who was gripping the big wheel with both hands.   He wondered if he should climb down. There was probably little he could do or even see up here during a storm. Yet the captain had sent him up so it would be up to the captain to call him down.

Glancing astern, he could still see the other two ships, but they seemed to have dropped off a little.

The advance wind hit with a rush and he turned into it. The rain quickly followed, and the ship disappeared below him. He pulled his cap down over his head and tied the string under his chin. The driving rain forced him to turn his face away and he slid down into the barrel as much as he could. Protecting his eyes with his hand, he watched as the following ships were swallowed up in the heavy rain. A blinding flash of lightning momentarily lit the scene below him, and then it was gone.

There was nothing he could see. The storm had pushed out what daylight remained, and it was already dark.

He huddled in misery, with his arms wrapped around himself, just wanting it to end, as the mast described wide swinging arcs in total submission to the broiling sea.

Water was beginning to build up in the barrel and his feet were already wet. Wrapping his coat tightly around himself, he bowed his head and waited. It was going to be a long night.

He thought of the last time he saw his father standing in the field as the ship left the harbour. He wondered if he would see him again. He hadn't thought about this happening when he had begged to go to sea. He wondered if he would have changed his mind if he had known. Probably not.

Pictures of Maria floated across his mind. He felt warmer. He listened to her voice in his head. It made him happy. He would be alright, he rationalized. The storm would pass. He just had to keep warm somehow. His whole body shook. He wondered if he could make it down to the deck. His head bobbed and he hit a glancing blow off the rim of the barrel. A small trickle of blood ran down his forehead and was quickly washed away by the rain. He closed his eyes and dropped his head onto his crossed arms.

25

Without warning the ship reared up on its stern and plunged down with a crash. Bo was thrown against the galley wall. Pots and pans littered the floor, spilling their contents as they rolled with the motion of the ship. He looked up from the floor to see Cook pushing to his knees near the stove. Blood smeared the edge of the cutting table where he had hit it as he was thrown to the floor. He rose to his knees and shook his head in confusion. The next wave knocked him to the floor again.

"Get that fire out," he mumbled to Bo from where he lay.

Bo scrambled across the floor on hands and knees to where the water barrel was lashed to the galley wall. The floor was wet where the water had sloshed over the edge. He dipped a small bucket and waited for the ship to begin its climb of the next wave. When he felt the front tilt to begin its rush down the other side he rushed across the floor, lifted the cover from the hot stove and dumped the contents of the bucket on the flames.

With an angry hiss the stove spat steam through the opening into Bo's face. Bo reared back and the ship ended its decent and crashed into the next wave, throwing him against the cutting table. He grabbed one of the thick legs and held on, the empty bucket slipping from his hands and clattering across the floor.

Cook grabbed the bucket as it bounced by him and threw it back to Bo.

"Better get another one to make sure it is all out," he said.

Bo retrieved the rolling bucket, released his grip on the table and let the momentum of the ship slide him across the floor to the barrel. He dipped the bucket a second time, rushed across the floor and dumped it through the opening in the stove, dousing the remaining embers.

Cook was still on his knees struggling to regain his feet. Blood trickled down his hairline near his ear. "Best get out of here," he muttered to Bo. "Won't be any hot food till this storm is over. I'll douse the candles."

Bo headed for the stairs, clinging to whatever he could hold, balancing the best he could against the violent thrashing of the ship. He wanted to get outside. He did not want to be trapped down here. He was terrified. Reaching the steps, he began to climb on his hands and knees. Fear gripped him and his stomach rolled. He had to get outside. The contents of his stomach spilled over the steps as the ship plunged again. His shoulder was throbbing from hitting the wall in the galley. Desperately he clawed his way to the small door in the hatch and pushed it open. The wind slammed it against the side of the hatch and rain washed over his upturned face. The shock of the sudden chill cleared his mind and he scrambled through onto the rain-slick deck. The roar of the wind drowned out any other sound.

He looped his arm through the guide rope attached to the raised sides of the hatch and looked around. The dark sea was thrashing itself about in a frenzy, doing its best to swamp the ship. They were at the storm's mercy, driven by rain-soaked wind that was turning the day into night.

He pulled hand over hand to the corner and peered around directly into the biting rain. Turning his face away he saw one of the small boats go tumbling across the deck, knocking down one of the sailors and pushing him against the rail.

With his hand sheltering his eyes, he watched three more of the men chase down the rolling boat. The ship reared again and threw them all against the mast, splintering the boat in pieces. One of the pieces was sticking out of the chest of the one they called Jorge.

He won't survive that, thought Bo. He looked up at the barrel near the top of the mast. The boy was up there. The barrel faded and disappeared as the rain suddenly grew heavier.

He would not be able to sleep outside tonight. In fact, he probably wouldn't sleep at all, not with the ship flailing about like this.

He moved out of the way as the sailors brought Jorge to the hatch and carried him down the steps. He followed them, closing the hatch door behind him, shutting out the howling wind and driving rain. Water dripped from his clothes, adding to the pools left behind by the sailors, some of them red with fresh blood. The ship tumbled them down the slick stairs in a tangle of arms and legs. With no protection, the ship managed to throw the limp body of Jorge ahead of the tumbling sailors, leaving him at the bottom of the steps underneath the others. The piece of splintered board was torn loose allowing the blood to spurt from the open wound onto his companions.

Bo watched from the corner as the sailors struggled across the food-covered floor and laid Jorge on one of the galley tables, lashed him down, and stepped back to make room for Cook. The dancing shadows from the newly lit candles revealed the look on Cook's face, telling Bo that Jorge would not be getting up from that table.

Cook lifted his head and met Bo's eyes across the room. "Get me some water," he said. "The rest of you get back on deck where you are needed."

Bo joined him at the table when the last of the sailors had disappeared up the stairs and the hatch door closed behind him.

Cook slid a knife underneath Jorge's blood-soaked tunic and split it top to bottom exposing the torn and pierced chest. With each labored breath the remaining splinters still embedded in the wound lifted and fell, frothy pink bubbles appeared and burst around its edge. Other than the rasping breaths, Jorge made no sound.

Bo and Cook anchored themselves to the table, balancing against the unpredictable motion of the ship. Cook soaked a rag in the bucket of water Bo held and washed the blood away as best he could. There was nothing else to be done. Bo smelled death in the room. He did not want to be there in the semi-dark galley with it, but he forced himself to stand there, on the opposite side of the table from Cook, watching as Jorge's breathing got weaker and eventually stopped.

"Get a piece of canvass to wrap him in," said Cook, breaking the silence. "Then clean up this mess on the floor."

26

They hadn't gone far when Meroobish, who had now been given the lead by Daygon, held up his hand and stopped on the trail. Turning around he whispered, "Do you smell that?"

The faint smell of wood smoke, carried on the light evening breeze, wafted across Daygon's nose. He smiled with satisfaction. The Shannok had done just what his brother had said they would.

"They are careless," Daygon whispered, as he waved the others to join them. "Go and take a closer look," he said to Meroobish.

Soundlessly, Meroobish weaved his way through the trees, quickly melting into their shadows. It always impressed Daygon that Meroobish, being such a large man, could move so easily and quietly through the thickest woods. It was something few of the other band members could do.

They all sat on the ground and waited in silence, their weapons held in their hands. The rattling water of the nearby river, occasionally accompanied by familiar night bird calls, were the only sounds. Each man was alone with his thoughts of the coming battle, never sure of its outcome but certain of its necessity in their roles as protectors of the band.

The silver glow above the distant trees heralded the soon arrival of the moon. It was going to be a bright night. That, with the lack of covering on the early spring trees, was going to make it difficult to get near the Shannok without being seen, regardless of their carelessness.

The only advantages they might have were the covering noise of the river and the fact that the Shannok weren't expecting to be followed.

Daygon didn't want any more of his men to be injured, so surprise was most important. He hoped it would be all over before the Shannok knew what was happening. He asked the Great Spirit to guide their way.

A startled night bird fluttered away from the trees into the night as Meroobish suddenly appeared in front of him, interrupting his thoughts. The look of concern on his face as he came closer alerted Daygon that all was not well. He raised his hand to quiet the murmured whispers of the men.

"What is it?" he whispered, as Meroobish reached the group now kneeling and crouching on the ground.

"Trouble," said Meroobish, as he settled on the ground next to Daygon.

"What kind of trouble?" asked Daygon, feeling the beginning of concern.

"It's an old camp. One of ours. There's a single mamateek there in a small clearing by the side of the river. It looks like an old couple were living in it. The old man is lying face down in the clearing. He's not moving. I think they killed him."

"Where's the old woman?" asked Bragadessh.

"They have her tied to a tree with a short piece of rope. She can move around a little, I think."

"Where are all the Shannok?"

"They are all around the fire, roasting fish from the old couple's supply."

"Where are their weapons?"

"Lying around the ground near them."

"Is there anyone on guard?"

"No. I counted them. They are all at the fire."

"Let's go," said Bragadessh.

"No," said Daygon, pointing up at the large round moon that had risen above the trees. "It is too bright. They will see us coming. We must wait until they fall asleep. That is the best time to take them."

"How big is the clearing?" he asked Meroobish.

"Not big. Maybe six or seven strides across."

"Is there much cover around the clearing?"

"Its mostly birch but there is some spruce."

"That should give us the cover we need."

"The river falls over some rocks at the side of the clearing, so there's plenty of noise," Meroobish added.

"Alright, Meroobish, you and Toorett go back and watch them. We will move up to the bend in the trail and wait. Try and make your way around to the other side of the clearing so that we can come at them from both directions. No one must escape."

Daygon and the others followed Meroobish and Toorett to the bend in the river, then watched as they continued down the trail and faded into the shadows of the trees.

They found dry ground at the side of the trail and settled in to wait. Soon he could hear low snoring noises of Modthamook, Pugathoite and Bragadessh. He could find no sleep and wondered how it was the others could be so relaxed in the face of the coming battle.

27

The first faint glow of daybreak found him still standing on the deck next to Fernam. The wind had ceased to rage, and the seas no longer broiled with fury. The ship had stopped fighting the rudder. His aching arms hung at his side. The long, exhausting night of helping Fernam hold the wheel was behind him.

Gaspar lifted his eyes to check the starry sky and discovered the ship had been blown off course, much further south than he had planned. He returned his weary eyes to the sea and scanned the horizon but saw nothing but water. The other two ships had disappeared from view in the storm. Tipping his head back again, he looked up the mast at the barrel. He could not see Paublo.

Returning his eyes to the lower deck, he scanned his ship. There seemed to be little damage other than the missing piece of rail, some tattered sails and the splintered rowboat. He was surprised and grateful. The storm had been one of his worst, but he had won. He wondered about his brother and Antonyo. They might not have fared so well.

"Go up there and check on the boy," he shouted to one of the men on the deck below. "Where's Bo? Get him to help."

28

Bo watched first light spread across the gray sky from his vantage point behind the hatch wall. He had tied a rope that had been secured to the safety lines on the raised hatch around his waist. The sea had finally stopped its thrashing and the rain had dwindled to showers. The ship had survived, and so had he.

It had been a long night. He had never been so terrified. He was sure the sea was going to take him. He did not want to die that way, not as a slave. He wanted to be a free man and die in his own land, with dignity.

All night he had stayed on deck in the shelter of the hatch wall, although it had done little to keep him dry. The panic that had gripped him below deck had subsided once he stepped outside, but it had been replaced with a disquieting fear of the approach of death. He could feel its presence near him and watched the darkness for it to appear. He was afraid to close his eyes.

The storm had repeatedly tossed him against the hatch wall so that he was bruised and cold when the light of day finally began to push the darkness aside. He thought maybe he had slept. He wasn't sure.

He looked behind the ship. The waves had died down. The wind no longer roared. He thought of the boy and looked up at the mast. Surely he could not have survived.

Hearing his name called, he pushed to his feet. "Go up and check on him, Bo," he heard the captain shout.

He untied the wet safety rope and joined one of the sailors at the rail. The sailor handed him a large coil of rope which he hung over his shoulder.

Together they swung out onto the ropes and began to climb. Men on the deck below had stopped their work and watched them as they made their way upward.

They reached the barrel and peered over the top. The boy was firmly wedged inside, his head resting on his arms.

"He's here, sir" the sailor shouted down to Gaspar. "Not sure if he's still alive, but he's here."

"Paublo, are you alright?" Bo asked.

The boy did not stir.

Certain he was dead, Bo lifted one arm and the sailor lifted the other to pull him out of the barrel. Paublo groaned softly. At first Bo thought it was the wind, but then there was a louder groan.

Taking the rope from his shoulder, he looped it over the yardarm and fastened it under Paublo's arms and across his chest.

29

It felt as though there was someone there with him. He thought he heard the faint sound of voices. One of them sounded like the African.

Were his knees were no longer drawn up to his chin? That couldn't be, he thought. His body shook with the cold. He felt like he was falling. "Maria", he whispered.

Bo and the sailor lifted Paublo from the barrel. Using the coil of rope, they slowly lowered him to the men waiting on the deck below.

Gaspar climbed down the steps and hurried to the group gathering around the motionless body on the main deck. Dropping to his knee in fear that he might have left him up there to die, he bent over the boy and touched his ice-cold cheek. He held the palm of his hand next to the boy's nose and lips and was relieved to feel the warm breath on his hand.

"He's still with us. Take him below and get him warmed up," he commanded.

Paublo opened his eyes just enough to see. There seemed to be people there in his blurred vision. He stared up into their faces as they slowly came into focus. He heard his name. His fingers and toes were tingling with cold. High above the faces he could see the sails. He wondered how he had reached the deck. Had he fallen? He felt no pain other than the cold. The rain no longer fell on his face.

Captain Gaspar bent over him and spoke. Paublo tried to smile, but his lips cracked and split. The taste of blood filled his mouth. He felt the captain's strong hand on his shoulder, and heard him say something.

As Gaspar began to push to his feet, Paublo's eyelids fluttered and opened. Through his cracked, bloody lips he croaked, "I did it, sir." Fresh blood trickled down his chin when he tried to smile. His heels lightly tapped the deck as his body began to shake from the cold.

Placing his hand on the boy's quivering chest, Gaspar smiled at him and replied, "You did, Paublo. You are good sailor. You did a good job and I thank you. Now go below and rest."

Turning to one of the sailors, he said, "Go up there and take his place. We have to find my other two ships."

Paublo closed his eyes and fought the pain as his blood began to find its way to his fingers and toes. He tried not to cry out.

Rough hands lifted him and carried him below deck.

It was warm outside the galley and there were food smells, good food smells.

30

Daygon had watched the moon slowly move across the sky, marking the passing of time. His ancestors had watched it with him, and he felt them close. The moon was now partially hidden by a large cloud that drifted across its face. He leaned back against the tree where he sat, smelling the pungent myrrh spilling from the bladder that had burst when his head rested against the trunk. He looked at the still forms of his brother and the other two where they slept with their hathemays and aaduths at their sides. He wished he could have slept too, but sleep never came easily to him when he was about to go into battle. He had known these men since they were boys, and now they were his responsibility and he hoped none of them got hurt in the coming battle. The Shannok were fierce warriors and couldn't be taken for granted, even if they were taken by surprise.

He had considered letting them go, but that wasn't the right thing to do. They had killed some of his men, and now had killed again. That could not be left unpunished. They must pay with their lives. That was the way. It had always been the way. It would be done at his hand before this night was over.

He thought of Shandowee, waiting with the others at the temporary camp on the trail. He wondered if she was awake. All he wanted was a peaceful life where they could raise their children without fear. He had no wish to fight, but these Shannok had brought this on themselves. Letting them go would only make them believe they could do whatever they wanted with his people. As chief, it was his responsibility to make sure they were punished and driven away from Beothuk land.

Looking up at the twinkling lights in the sky, he smiled at his many ancestors up there watching him. They were his protectors, the ones who had gone before him. Some day he would join them, but he hoped this would not be the night. He hoped he would see many nights before that. He wanted to be there for his family, to watch his children grow.

Next to him, Bragadessh stirred and murmured softly, "Is it time, brother?"

"It is. Wake the others, and we will prepare to go."

Bragadessh pushed to his knees, lightly touched each of the other two men on the shoulder, and they were instantly awake. Quietly they gathered around Daygon, squatting on the ground with their weapons in their hands.

"This thing we do tonight we do for our band," he began. "Our families are counting on us to protect them. You were picked because you are our people's best warriors. These Shannok murdered our people. It is up to us to punish them and send a warning to others who may consider coming here to do the same. It is time for them to die."

His three men nodded in agreement. He could see the nervous anticipation in their eyes in the muted light of the moon. He knew he could count on each one of them. They had seen battle together before.

"We will kill them in their sleep. Make no sound until we are all in position," Daygon instructed.

"What about the old woman?" asked Pugathoite.

"Protect her from the Shannok. They will probably be too busy defending themselves to worry about her."

31

Rui, Paublo's replacement, reached the barrel and swung his legs over the edge, quickly discovering he was not built for the new lookout. He was much taller than Paublo and standing in the narrow barrel the rim only reached halfway up his chest. He considered climbing out and standing on the yardarm as he had many times before, but the barrel gave him more security, so he stayed.

Shielding his eyes with his hand to his forehead, he scanned the empty sea, slowly making a complete circle of the ship. Well off to starboard he thought he spotted something, but it disappeared, so he continued his circle. Returning to the spot again, he squinted, straining his eyes. There it was again! A tiny white speck at the very end of his vision. He stared at it until he was sure and then shouted down to Gaspar on the deck below, "Sail on the horizon."

"Where?" Gaspar shouted through cupped hands.

"Off the starboard side," shouted Rui, pointing over the stern of the ship.

"Turn the ship around," ordered Gaspar. "It must be one of ours. Let's find out which one."

Sailors scrambled up the ropes and hurriedly trimmed the sails. The ship took a wide sweeping turn and soon they were underway in the direction Rui had pointed, retracing their course.

Gaspar stood at the rail, straining his tired eyes, trying his best to make out the tiny white speck in the distance. He hoped it was Miguel, but it was too far away to tell. Like most of his men, he had not slept nor eaten in a day. Tacking against the wind it would take hours, to reach the tiny sail on the horizon. He decided to go below to his cabin. Although he expected he probably wouldn't sleep, he knew he could not go on without some rest.

Before leaving the wheel deck he ordered half his men to do the same. Fernam surrendered the wheel to his replacement and he and Gaspar walked down the stairs together.

As he stepped on the main deck, he turned and called to his first mate, "Come get me as soon as we are near them," he ordered, nodding toward the far away ship. "And get that wreckage cleaned up."

32

The throbbing pain in the tips of his fingers and toes as the blood began to circulate again was unbearable. He moaned and squirmed with the unrelenting agony. Tears escaped from the corner of his eyes and trickled down his wind-burned cheeks. He screwed his eyes shut and bit down on his already cracked and bleeding lips. The salty taste of blood filled his mouth.

He felt a hand resting on his chest, and opened his eyes to stare up into the dark eyes of Bo. There was kindness in their depths. He tried to smile through his blood-crusted lips at the African and winced at the pain.

"You will be alright now," said Bo. "The storm is over."

The sound of his voice was comforting. He was too tired to speak. He just wanted to sleep.

As he turned his head to the side, the flickering candles illuminated a canvass-wrapped form on the other galley table.

Wondering what had happened and who it was, he closed his eyes and slept.

Maria walked toward him from out of the shadows.

33

Just ahead, the river changed to rapids where the water had cut its way through a small hillside. It was much noisier here and Daygon turned and placed his hand over his mouth signalling complete silence. He knew his men understood that talking here would carry a great distance because of the tendency to talk over the noise of the river, but he thought a reminder was warranted. Each man nodded in turn.

Daygon turned and followed the footpath up the small incline that skirted the rapids. At the top Daygon had a view of the valley below and, in the distance, he could see the faint glow of a fire. His heart began to beat faster. The time was near now. He turned and grinned at Bragadessh. His hand gripped his aaduth a little tighter. He felt a quickening in his steps as he led his companions down the side of the hill toward the Shannok camp.

As they neared the edge of the clearing, Daygon gave a soft whistle, mimicking an evening bird, to alert Meroobish and

Toorett. The answering call followed and Toorett materialized out of the semi-darkness.

"Meroobish is hiding in the trees on the other side of the clearing," he whispered, as he joined the group. "See that group of spruce on the other side of the fire? He's in there."

From cover of a large spruce tree, Daygon looked across the small clearing. The soft glow of the dying embers of the Shannok's fire highlighted their sleeping shapes. A little removed from them, he spotted the old woman sitting with her back against the tree she was tied to.

"Should we free her first?" asked Bragadessh, nodding toward the old woman.

"Probably not. She might be safer where she is," Daygon replied. "Everyone keep low and spread out once you get in the clearing. The moon is still giving plenty of light."

"Wait," hissed Toorett, grabbing Daygon's arm. "Look," he said pointing toward the fire.

One of the Shannok had pushed to his feet. He looked around the darkened woods, tossed several sticks on the firepit, and walked to the far side of the clearing. Standing with his feet splayed apart, he began to relieve himself, directing the stream into the low underbrush.

Kneeling on the ground, Daygon watched a large shadow slowly rise from the bushes to the Shannok's left. Meroobish soundlessly stepped up behind the unsuspecting Shannok and covered his mouth with his hand as he plunged his knife deep into his back.

That leaves four, Daygon thought as he heard the muffled grunt. He motioned to his men and they left the cover of the bushes and began to crawl across the hardened, open ground toward the now flickering fire that had found new life.

They had just reached the body of the old man lying face down near the edge of the clearing when the old woman, alerted by the Shannok's grunt, spotted them and began to yell.

"Over here. Save me," she screamed. "Save me. They killed my husband. They're going to kill me. Save me." The volume of the screams escalated, shattering the quiet of the night, sending frightened birds and animals fluttering and scurrying into the night.

The five Beothuk froze on their knees, exposed to the Shannok at the fire who had been roused from their sleep by the old woman's shouts. One of them spotted the Beothuk and sounded the alarm in that strange language. Daygon did not understand the words but he knew the meaning.

"Now," he yelled, as he scrambled to his feet.

Daygon saw the dark shape of Meroobish coming from the other side of the clearing, as he began to run at the closest Shannok. At his side he sensed Bragadessh release an arrow and saw it hit the chest of one of the other Shannok who had not yet made it to his feet. He fell backwards into the fire, his clothing quickly igniting. The sudden flare lit the small clearing making it as light as day. His screams added to the confusion and fear of the other Shannok who were scrambling for their weapons.

Daygon pushed on toward his target, lifting his aaduth over his head as he ran. The Shannok released an arrow that touched his ear in passing. He heard Toorett, who was running behind him, grunt in pain. Swinging his arm, he sent the aaduth in an arc and saw it embed itself in the Shannok's chest. The bow slipped from his fingers as he fell to his knees gripping the shaft of the aaduth with both hands before falling over on his side.

To his left he saw Meroobish dispense another Shannok who had made the mistake of thinking he could win a hand to hand fight with just a knife.

The Shannok who was on fire was on his knees screaming wildly as he tried to beat out the flames that engulfed him. Daygon noticed he had bloody rags wrapped around his leg.

To Daygon's right, Bragadessh was wrestling on the ground with a knife wielding Shannok. Modthamook came to his rescue, dealing a fatal blow with his short axe, retrieved from the back of the Shannok with the shaft of Daygon's aaduth protruding from his chest.

The moans from the burning Shannok finally subsided and all was quiet. The smell of burnt flesh drifted across the clearing.

The old woman began her yelling again.

Daygon looked back at Toorett who was sitting on the ground with an arrow sticking from his left shoulder. "Are you alright?" he asked.

"I am," Toorett grunted. "It will heal once this stick is pulled out."

"Move closer to the fire," he said.

Meroobish grabbed the heels of the burned Shannok and dragged him to the edge of the clearing.

"Take all their heads," said Daygon, "and someone release the old woman and make her stop that screaming."

Kneeling next to Toorett, who was now sitting next to the fire, he said, "We have to pull the arrow out."

"I know," groaned Toorett.

Bragadessh threw more wood on the fire, sending a shower of sparks skyward.

"Do you have something to treat this with?" Daygon asked the old woman as she approached, still mumbling obscenities about the Shannok.

"I do," she hissed, and spit on one of the dead Shannok as she passed him on the way to her mamateek.

"Hold him down," Daygon said to Meroobish.

Meroobish gripped Toorett's arms pinning them against the ground. Daygon gave Toorett a stick to bite down on as he gripped the shaft of the arrow. It had not gone all the way through and the Shannok were not using arrow heads, so it had to be pulled back out.

Without further warning he dropped his knee against Toorett's chest and yanked. The arrow came free, followed by a spurt of blood that quickly subsided to a slow trickle. Toorett's body stiffened, his teeth ground into the stick and he moaned with pain.

The old woman pushed the men aside and coated the wound with a paste she brought from the mamateek. Then she wrapped Toorett's shoulder.

"You'll make it son," she said with a toothless grin.

34

Gasper stepped down off the last step onto the main deck and wearily followed Fernam to the main hatch where they took the ladder down to the galley level. Every muscle ached and his eyelids were heavy with fatigue, but he hadn't been able to check on Jorge until now and he'd received no report since the accident.

He hoped his best carpenter had survived, but he feared what he was about to find. The wood that had pierced his chest had not been small. It may have gone too deep to be repaired.

At the bottom of the ladder they met Bo coming from the galley, carrying a cask in his arms. The cooking smells that followed him out the door were a powerful reminder to Gaspar that he hadn't eaten in a long time. His mouth filled with saliva and his stomach rumbled in anticipation. He wasn't sure which he needed more, food or sleep. He felt he might collapse from lack of either.

"Where's Jorge?" asked Gaspar.

"Cook has him back there behind the galley, Cap'n. He's next to young Paublo."

Gaspar followed Bo to the end of the galley wall. Rounding the corner, he found two of the tables with bodies on them. One was wrapped in a blood-stained sail, the other was the sleeping form of young Paublo. Cook watched from the door, wiping his hands with the tail of his stained apron.

Cook met Gaspar's eyes. "He didn't make it, sir," he said. "We did everything we could. He just lost too much blood. There was no savin' him. That plank just made too big a hole in his chest."

Gaspar removed his hat. Looking at the dark stains that covered the planks underneath the table, he nodded and said, "Thank you, Cook. Finish getting him ready and we will bury him later today. We will give him back to the sea he loved."

"Yes sir. He did love being on the water. It was where he was most happy."

Bone weary, Gaspar left the galley, made his way back up the stairs and across the deck to his quarters. Before stepping through the door, he glanced toward the horizon where he could see the tiny speck that might be Manual or Antonyo's ship. It was still going to take hours to get there. Tiredly, he pushed the door fully open and stepped inside.

Before falling on his bed, he took down the logbook and made a note of Jorge's passing. He would have to take the news to his wife when they returned to Terceira, he thought as he fell asleep, letting the book slide through his fingers to the cabin floor.

35

The sun had cleared the distant trees and painted the hillside yellow by the time Daygon opened his eyes. Last night he had slept well. There had been no dreams. His mind had been free of worry. The battle was over. The victory was theirs. He felt the band would be safe again. Now they could return to the life they had come to the coast to live.

Bragadessh and Meroobish were sitting near the fire roasting some fish from the old couple's store. Bragadessh turned as Daygon pushed to a sitting position. Holding up the stick with the skewered fish, he said, "Come brother, it's time to eat. Time for sleeping is past."

The sun climbed in the sky as they sat around the fire enjoying the roasted fish. The conversation was light and easy. The tension of the fight with the Shannok was past. Their remains had been dragged to the edge of the clearing and disposed of in the bushes. The animals would deal with the rest. Only their heads remained. They would be taken care of before they left camp.

"How's that shoulder?" Daygon asked Toorett after the meal was done.

"It's sore but I'll live," he replied with a grin.

"We'd best take care of the old man," Daygon said as he pushed to his feet. "We should be getting back to the band."

They scooped a shallow grave from the dirt near the mamateek and placed the stiffened body in it. River stones were brought and placed over the top of the dirt to protect him and to mark his place.

Daygon convinced the old woman to accompany them back to where the band was waiting. He promised her she would have protection there.

Before leaving the clearing, they cut five poles and stuck them in the ground at the river's edge, each mounted with a Shannok's head facing downstream. It would serve as a warning to others and hopefully keep them away from this part of the river.

Daygon had delayed their departure to the temporary camp to allow Toorett to rest. The sun had climbed high in the sky before they started the return trip. It took much longer than it should have, due to the old woman's refusal to rush, demands for frequent rests, and constant complaining. Daygon was regretting having persuaded her to come with them.

When they reached the place where the first battle had taken place, they built two hand slides and lashed the bodies of Assonwitt and Bashoodite to them. Meroobish pulled one and Bragadessh the other.

The sun had almost completed its journey and sat low in the sky when they finally walked into the temporary camp, pulling the slides containing their band member's bodies. Toorett walked at the front, with the head of the Shannok from the first battle dangling from the hand of his good arm.

Odusweet's haunting wails of despair alerted the rest of the camp that the warriors had returned, and that all was not well.

36

It must have been the knock at his door that startled him, tugging him back from the deep sleep he had thought would not come.

"Enter," he mumbled sleepily, as shredded scenes of the rolling green and yellow hills of Terceira floated away into the mist of his dream.

Bo pushed the door open, ducking his head to avoid hitting it on the heavy timber door header. In one hand he carried a metal tray balancing a steaming cup and a plate containing a thick sandwich. The strong smell of the coffee filled the quarters, triggering the saliva in Gaspar's mouth. He remembered he hadn't eaten last night after visiting Jorge.

"We are close to the ship now, sir," said Bo. "Cook says you have to eat this before going on deck."

Gaspar smiled. "Cook is giving me orders now, is he Bo?"

"Yas sir. I s'pect he is, sir. Mostly gives everyone orders, sir." Bo replied. "He says you haven't eaten in a day, sir." Bo laid the tray on the table.

Gaspar swung his legs out over the cot and held out his hand for the coffee that Bo was handing him. He took a moment to enjoy the feeling of the hot liquid as it trickled down his throat, warming him from within.

Bo picked up the open logbook from the floor and placed it on the table next to the tray.

"How's Paublo?" Gaspar asked, as he took his first bite of the sandwich.

"He's up and around again, sir. Seems almost good as new."

"Probably rearing to get back up in the barrel," said Gaspar, as he washed the bite of sandwich down with a gulp of coffee.

"Probably is, sir. Seems to like it up there. If he made it through that storm, I s'pect he can make it through anything."

Gaspar pushed to his feet and began changing his clothes. As soon as he was ready, he picked up the rest of the sandwich and mug of coffee and stepped through the door. He downed the remaining coffee and ate the rest of the sandwich as he walked to the stairs leading up to the wheel deck. Bo padded silently along behind him waiting for the empty mug.

The wind had all but died, as if the storm had hooked it and dragged it away. The sun had cleared the horizon. He had slept the night away he realized; much longer than he had expected. He felt much better. The sleep had served him well.

Out on the starboard side a ship was almost in hailing distance. He was disappointed to see it was only one and it wasn't his brother's.

Looking over the damaged ship, it was obvious it had taken more of a hit from the storm than his had. The main mast had cracked about ten feet from the top and was dangling over the tattered sail. Several sailors were in the ropes cutting away the shredded sail and splintered mast with hatchets.

He scanned the sea for Miguel's ship but saw nothing. Looking up to the barrel he bellowed the question, "See anything?"

"Nothing, sir," came back the reply.

"Lower a boat," he commanded. "I'm going over there." He nodded to Fernam who had reclaimed his position behind the wheel. "Keep her close," he said.

"Aye, sir."

The rowboat was lowered and a crew of four rowers climbed down the rope ladder and jumped aboard. Gaspar followed and manned the tiller himself. The now quiet sea allowed them to cross the gap between the two ships in good time.

Gaspar surveyed the damage as they pulled alongside. Beside the broken mast, two sections of the rail on the port side were missing, leaving raw, splintered ends behind. *One of the row boats must have gone through there,* he thought.

His friend, Captain Antonyo, stood at the rail looking down at him as he swung onto the rope ladder and scrambled up the side of the ship.

"Welcome aboard, Gaspar," he said, holding out his hand to help him onto the deck.

Gaspar nodded. He stood for a minute looking over the tangled mess on the deck. "You seemed to have fared a little worse than I did," he commented. "Did you lose anyone?"

"Two good men," Antonyo replied, nodding toward the splintered rail. "The sea took them. There was nothing we could do once they went overboard."

"I lost two also," Gaspar said grimly.

"It's the price the sea exacted," mumbled Antonyo. "She always has to have her payment.

"Have you seen Miguel's ship?"

"He was close to us during the early part of the storm. I don't think he is far away. We couldn't keep lookouts up there on the yardarm, so we lost sight of him when the storm got worse."

"Where did you see him last?"

"He was behind us, to port"

Gaspar turned back to look at his own ship and beckoned to Rui, who was standing in the barrel, to scan the sea behind them.

To Antonyo he said, "We've lost a day, and four men, and we have been pushed to the south with this storm. I think we will continue on this course once we find Miguel. There is a better chance of finding good timbers to repair the damage. The land we found last year was frozen and barren. The few trees were stunted and bent. Nothing that would serve as a mast. How is she handling?"

"She's in better shape than she looks. We will manage. Might be a little slower but she is still plenty seaworthy."

Gaspar walked to the rail to where the rowboat waited. "I will sail back that way and look for him," he said, pointing over the stern. "You keep us in sight."

"I will. Good luck, Gaspar."

"Join me in my cabin for supper tonight," said Gaspar, as he began to climb down the rope ladder. "Hopefully Miguel will be there as well."

37

Assonwitt and Bashoodite were carried along the path, a short distance from the main clearing where the rest of the band was gathered. Temporary shelters were built for their families and they were left to stay with the bodies for the night. The band members then returned to the main clearing to prepare for the celebration of the victory over the Shannok. Preparation of Assonwitt and Bashoodite for their burial and journey to Gossett (land of the dead) was left for the next day. That was a ceremony for the light of day, and it was necessary now to give thanks and celebrate the battle they had just won.

Despite the loss to the band, there was an air of anticipation. The Great Spirit had provided them the means to defeat their enemy. He would surely keep them safe for the remainder of the season. Daygon watched their faces as they busied themselves for the celebration. There was relief and a sense of promise in the way they laughed and smiled as they worked together. Even the children had gone back to their games, adding to the air of festivity with their shouts and laughter as they ran around the clearing, getting in the way more often than not. He felt good. They had done the right thing in hunting down the Shannok. He hoped they would always be able to drive the intruders away from their land and keep it the way it was now for their children.

Wood was gathered and a fire was built in the center of the clearing. Large river stones were brought from the river and placed in a ring around the fire. Once the fire had heated them up, fish and meat were dropped on them to cook.

Then the story telling of the battle began as the hot food was grabbed from the stones and passed around. Some of the warriors stood and danced around the fire, re-enacting the battle to shouts of encouragement and praise for their great feats from the listeners.

The head of the Shannok was mounted on a pole near the centre of the clearing and the whole band danced around it, shouting thanks to the Great Spirit for giving them the victory over their enemy. Outside the circle children danced and shouted, mimicking the warriors, trying their best to out-shout their friends.

Daygon leaned against a birch tree at the edge of the clearing watching the celebration. He had watched this celebration many times before. He knew it was a release for his people and was something they needed to move past the loss of Assonwitt and Bashoodite. It gave meaning to their sacrifice. Tomorrow they would be honored as they began their journey to Gossett.

Long afterwards, when the fire had died to glowing embers and most of the women and children were strewn around the clearing asleep where they lay, the discussion turned to where they should make camp, and whether it was safe to continue on to the coast.

Some of those who spoke thought they should make camp where they were and send groups to the coast to gather food. There was more danger at the coast, they felt.

Others argued that this would add too much time to the activity and would put them at risk of not gathering enough food for the snow season. It would also expose small groups to the possibility of attack on the daily trek from the coast to the camp. They thought it was better to make camp at the coast and keep everyone together. There was safety in numbers they reasoned. The Shannok would not bother such a large group.

Daygon listened quietly to all the arguments, giving everyone who wished to talk the chance to speak their mind. It was the only way he could get to understand how the band felt. He felt it was always necessary to have as much information as possible before making a decision.

At the end, when the fire had all but died, the eyes of the others turned to him and he began to speak.

"Many good arguments have been made," he began. "Those who wish to stay here do so out of fear of the Shannok. I understand those fears, and do not wish to take you to the coast where you believe there is a greater danger from them. What you must remember is the Great Spirit has seen fit to give us a great victory over them and they will not trouble us again this season. Setting up camp at the coast will make it a lot easier to gather the food we must have for the snow season. I believe that is the best choice."

After a few moments some of those sitting around the dying fire began to nod their agreement. It was the wisest choice, they agreed.

"Good," said Daygon. "We will leave tomorrow after we have buried our friends."

"When we reach the coast, we will mount the head of the Shannok near the water to warn them away and, if they do not heed it, we have sufficient numbers to take care of any attack by them. Some of the older boys can watch the camp and warn of the approach of any intruders."

This seemed to ease the concern of the few who were holding out and they expressed their acceptance of the plan.

"Thank you," said Daygon, with relief. He had worried about leaving some of the band behind. He leaned back on his arms and looked up at the twinkling lights high above. It seemed as if his ancestors were telling him it was going to be alright.

Pushing to his feet, he headed toward the temporary shelter he had built, feeling happy with what the band had decided. Looking up at the twinkling lights far above he acknowledged his ancestors and asked them to petition the Great Spirit for protection for the band.

Ducking under the spruce boughs forming the sloped roof, he lay down next to the dark form lying on the ground. It will be a good season despite this trouble, he thought, as he wrapped his arms around his sleeping wife and the little bundle cradled in her arms.

38

While they had been on Antonyo's ship the wind had begun to blow again. The sailors struggled against the oars on the return trip to Gaspar's ship. Standing in the stern, Gaspar had to keep a firm grip on the tiller to stay on his feet. The water coming over the side of the boat sloshed around his boots, making the floorboards treacherously slippery. As they neared the ship, two of the sailors used their oars to fend off their boat as the waves tried to throw them against the side, threatening to smash the little rowboat. On the deck above them, sailors draped heavy ropes over the side to help cushion the blows as others swung the boom out over them. The dangling ropes were grabbed by the rowers and tied to the boat and the deck crew hoisted them from the water. Once clear, the boat was swung onto the deck and Gaspar and his companions jumped out.

Gaspar ran up the stairs to the wheel deck and immediately ordered them to turn around and head in the direction Antonyo had told him he had last seen Miguel. The sails billowed and snapped in protest as the ship came around onto the new course and tacked into the wind once again.

Gaspar watched over the stern rail as they began to pull away from Antonyo's ship limping along behind them. The damaged ship seemed to be holding its own against the sea, even though the speed was greatly reduced. He turned his gaze forward again, straining to see sails on the horizon.

He and Miguel did not always see eye to eye, and Gaspar knew it was a sore point with Miguel that his younger brother had been given leadership of this exploration. That was the choice of the king, not him, though he doubted that made any difference to Miguel.

The three ships were his responsibility and he needed to find the lost one. The fact that it was his brother's ship made it all the more urgent. He would not want to face his family if his brother was not found.

Having to tack across the wind wasn't making it any easier and it delayed them from getting back to where Antonyo had told him he had last seen Miguel's ship. Gaspar paced the deck in agitation, glowering at the helmsman every time the ship lost way against the head wind.

An hour slowly dragged by and then another, and then the cry he was waiting for came from the lookout, "sail on the starboard side."

Seeing nothing from the deck, Gaspar swung out onto the ropes and clambered up to where Rui stood in the small barrel.

Shading his eyes, he scanned the horizon where Rui was pointing. His heart leaped when the tiny dot came into focus and formed into the shape of a sail as he squinted his eyes against the wind. It was too far away to know if it was Miguel, but he expected it was. He didn't expect to find anyone else out here. The fact that sails were visible meant the ship was underway and probably hadn't been severely damaged by the storm. He glanced behind and was pleased to see that Antonyo had been able to keep in sight.

"Keep an eye on them," he ordered, as he turned back and stared at the tiny spot on the horizon.

"Aye, sir. Won't take my eyes off them, sir."

Gaspar nodded and began the climb back down to the deck.

"Let's get more speed out of her," he shouted, as he swung onto the deck from the wet, slippery ropes. Running up the ladder to the wheel deck, he pointed in the direction in which he had spotted the ship, showing Fernam who was manning the wheel again.

"Let's go get my brother," he said with a grin, as Fernam spun the big wheel and the taut sails groaned against the ropes. The sudden change in direction tilted the ship sharply, sending sheets of spray washing over the lower deck, until it regained its footing and righted itself.

Holding to the rail, Gaspar watched the handling of the ship with appreciation. He had a good ship and a good crew. This would still turn out to be a good voyage. Of this he was certain.

39

By the sound of the activity outside, it was clear many in the camp were already awake when Daygon pushed aside the caribou skins covering him and Shandowee. Little Gadedoo was sleeping between them and had not yet stirred. Shandowee looked at Daygon and smiled as she watched his lingering gaze at their son.

Daygon leaned across Gadedoo and kissed her lightly on the lips.

"You are my sun," he whispered, and pushed to his feet.

Stepping outside the temporary shelter of evergreen branches, he stretched and yawned extensively. The morning sun had climbed above the distant hills and was spreading a golden hue over everything it touched. He liked this season with the warmth of the sun turning everything green again.

Last night's fire was now only a gray heap in the center of the little clearing, the dry ash swirling in the gentle gusts of the light breeze.

On the other side of the clearing Modthamook emerged from the woods, followed by two of the women carrying large sheaths of birch rind in their arms. They walked to where Odusweet and several other women were washing the bodies of Assonwitt and Bashoodite, and dropped the bundles on the ground next to them.

A large container of red ochre was brought to them, and when they had finished weaving fresh braids in the warrior's long hair the women began to paint the bodies. Once the bodies were completely covered with the red ochre the women rolled them on their sides, tucked the birch rind sheaths underneath and lay them flat. A second sheath was then used to cover them. Using thin roots, they tied the birch rind together and these coverings were then painted with the ochre as well.

Daygon sat with his brother watching the women work. He had seen this before and knew how important it was to properly prepare the bodies for their journey and the unknown perils they might encounter on their way.

Atop a small grass-covered hill that overlooked the river, several men were on their knees carving shallow holes in the earth.

When the women were finished their preparations, Daygon helped carry the bodies to the hilltop, followed by a long procession that included everyone in the band. Most of the adults were softly singing the burial song as they walked. At the top of the hill the two friends were lifted from the shoulders of their carriers and gently laid in the shallow graves, side by side, with their backs slightly elevated so they could watch the activity on the river. Their weapons, an aaduth for Assonwitt and a hathemay and arrows for Bashoodite, had also been coated with red ochre, and were placed next to them to honor them as warriors and to give them protection in their journey to Gossett. River stones that had been previously gathered were placed over the thin layer of earth covering the two men.

Many of the men stepped to the front of the group and told stories of their friends' bravery in battle, and their contributions to their families and the band. The sun had completed much of its journey across the sky when the last story was spoken, and everyone returned to their temporary shelters.

The fire at the center of the camp was rebuilt and a caribou was roasted over it. Everyone shared in the meat as the ceremony continued.

The celebrations only stopped when the sun had disappeared below the trees, and evening darkness had crept across the clearing.

"Assonwitt and Bashoodite will have a safe journey," said Daygon to Bragadessh and Meroobish. "Soon they will join our ancestors up there," he continued, indicating the twinkling lights far above them.

"We will join them some day," Bragadessh replied.

"Not too soon I hope," muttered Meroobish as his lips pulled back over his protruding teeth in a wide grin. "I have much life to live yet."

Daygon and Bragadessh chuckled softly and nodded at their friend as he leaned forward and tossed another stick on the fire, kicking up a spray of flankers that floated away into the night, quickly swallowed by the darkness.

40

The closer they drew to the ship the more certain he became that it was Miguel's, and he finally stopped pacing the deck. The gap closed quickly now that the ships were sailing toward each other. Scanning the structure of his brother's approaching ship, it didn't appear to Gaspar that it had suffered any damage from the storm.

He watched as the ship was brought around and headed in the same direction as his. A rowboat was lowered and rowed to the side of his ship and he waited for his brother to reach the rail and swing over onto the deck. They embraced in a lingering bear hug.

"It is good to see you, brother," laughed Gaspar, as he pushed him out to arms length.

"And you, Gaspar."

"That was a heavy storm."

"How did Antonyo fare?" asked Miguel, looking at the other ship in the distance. "He doesn't seem to have full sails."

"He took the worst of it. The top of his main mast was broken off.

"Did he lose anyone?"

"Two of his men, one of them his lookout. I lost two men as well. Jorge was impaled with splintered wood from one of the row boats that got loose. He died later, below decks."

"We came through it alright. Just lost sight of Antonyo's ship when the rain came. Glad to see he made it."

"We've been driven south of our course from last year. I think we'll stay on this one until we make landfall and find some timbers to repair Antonyo's mast. We can decide where to go from there."

"Probably the best plan. There wasn't much in the way of timbers on the land we saw last year."

"Have you eaten?"

"Haven't eaten or slept much in the last couple of days."

"Come to my cabin. We'll have Antonyo join us when we get close enough. I'll get Cook to put something on for us."

"Have Cook bring us some food," Gaspar shouted to Bo who was standing near the forward hatch. "Captain Antonyo will be here as well."

Bo nodded and hurried down the hatchway stairs.

Gaspar put his arm around his brother's shoulder, and they headed across the deck to the door of his quarters.

41

The next day Daygon supervised the breaking of camp. He was anxious to get the band to the coast where the gathering of food for the long snow season would take place. There was much work to be done and they had already lost enough time with this encounter with the Shannok. It was time to get the coastal camp set up and the band settled for the warm season.

He helped Shandowee repack their belongings and lifted the heavy carrying rack to her shoulders. Then Daygon did a walk around the temporary camp encouraging the band members to finish their preparations and get on the trail.

He assigned Meroobish, Modthamook and Pugathoite to scout ahead of the main procession to ensure there was no repeat of the earlier Shannok attack. Shortly after the three of them left camp, the band began to assemble and set out on the river trail that wound its way to the coast.

Daygon stood and watched them pass. These were his charges. They had selected him to lead them because they believed he would protect them. The empty eyes of the Shannok's head stared at him from atop the pole at the center of the clearing, a reminder of the dangers that might still lurk in their future.

He felt a slight pressure as Shandowee's arm slipped around his waist, and he looked down into her eyes, bright with love and understanding.

"It will be alright, my husband," she said with a smile and a reassuring squeeze of her arm.

A sudden catch deep in his chest made him lean into her and kiss her gently on her soft lips.

Dropping down on one knee, he lifted Gadedoo and placed him astride his shoulders. Smiling at Shandowee, he turned and followed the last family as they passed by.

42

Paublo made his way up the galley stairs to the deck. The pain in his hands and feet was only a memory now. Looking up through the open hatchway door his eyes were met by thousands of twinkling lights surrounding the silver glow of a full moon. It was the first night he had seen since the storm. The thought occurred to him Maria might be looking at the same sky. He tried to find a star he could show her when he returned.

Stepping over the threshold, he walked around the corner to where Bo was sitting with his back against the hatch wall. He took a seat on the deck next to him. The lights of the other two ships were a short distance behind them.

"You better now, boy?" asked Bo.

"I am. The pain is finally all gone."

"You see those lights up there?" said Bo, pointing skyward.

"Yes."

"That's the same lights I looked at when I was a boy."

Paublo leaned his head back against the hatch wall and stared at the dark sky, sprinkled with hundreds of pin pricks of twinkling lights.

"We must be getting close to my home now if I can see those lights."

Paublo looked at Bo in the muted darkness. "Tell me about your home, Bo," he said quietly.

"It is a beautiful place," Bo began in his rich African voice. "Much warmer than here. The animals and birds are different there. We have elephants that are many, many, times bigger than your horses. We have lions that are fierce and dangerous. And then there are the monkeys. They are afraid of no one and they steal everything. In the rivers there are crocodiles. They can bite a man in half with their jaws."

It was the most Paublo had heard Bo say since he had met him. "What about your family?"

"I have a grandson there, maybe your age. He is with his mother. His father was killed when they came and took us from our village."

"What is his name?"

"Kelanti. That is his name."

"That's a strong name."

"It is. It means swift river. He is the man of our family now, until I get back. They took all the men from the village."

Paublo considered telling Bo they were going away from Africa, but then why kill his dream, he rationalized. He felt closer to Bo than anyone else on the ship. He wondered if he was doing the right thing letting him believe this. What could it hurt? He would eventually find out anyway.

"I will show you some day," said Bo, interrupting his thoughts."

"That would be nice," Paublo replied. "I would love to see your place."

Two sailors stepped out of the hatch. As they walked past the closest one spat a stream of tobacco juice on the deck next to Bo's feet.

"Clean that up, boy," he said, with a loud laugh to his companion as they continued around the corner of the wall.

"Yes, sir," said Bo, as he pushed to his knees and pulled out the soiled rag that was dangling from his back pocket.

Paublo looked at the backs of the sailors as they disappeared around the corner. He felt sorry for Bo, but he was the captain's slave. It wasn't his place to interfere. He hoped someday Bo did find his freedom, and he hoped he was there to see it.

He pushed to his feet and looked up at the barrel high up on the mast. "I'll be back up there tomorrow, Bo," he said, as he turned and went below.

Bo watched him go, a half smile on his dark face.

43

The dawn sun was still hidden below the horizon when Paublo began his climb to the barrel. Faint traces of white spilled over the edge, coloring the dark water where it touched the sky. As he climbed higher the tip of the sun appeared, washing the horizon with shafts of gold and yellow. Another day had begun.

The other two ships were in line astern. He scanned the sea all the way around. There was nothing more to see. *The sea is a lot calmer than it was the last time I was here,* he thought.

He couldn't remember much about that ordeal. After the wall of rain hit, drawing a curtain over the rest of the world, he mostly kept his head down below the barrel rim. At first, he'd occasionally peered over the rim at the wild storm that was effortlessly tossing the ship around, more from a sense of duty than anything else. But he soon realized the futility of that. Day had suddenly turned to night and he couldn't see more than a few feet anyway. He pushed as far down in the barrel as he could, trying to wedge himself tight to ensure he wasn't thrown out by the unpredictable and erratic swinging of the mast that was being tossed around like a blade of grass caught in the swirl of a summer breeze. It was terrifying. He was soaked, bitterly cold, and bruised. He had thought that he would not make it through the night. Finally, in resignation he tucked his head down on his updrawn knees and began to repeat Maria's name over and over again until she came to him in his dream.

Paublo looked down to the deck and spotted Diego, one of the soldiers the captain had brought, standing at the starboard rail. Of all the men on the ship, Diego seemed to have the strongest dislike for Bo. Paublo had seen it on his face and in the way he treated Bo. Most of the men treated him as the slave he was, with no rights or privileges of any kind. Diego treated him with disgust, as if his very presence offended him.

Diego was the shortest man in the crew. Paublo suspected he tried to make up for it by bullying, and Bo was the obvious target. If Bo hadn't been on the ship, he suspected he would have been Diego's target. *Perhaps I should be thankful for that*, he thought.

Every chance Diego got he would push Bo around and belittle him, especially if he had an audience.

Yesterday he had deliberately tripped Bo as he was carrying the tray of dirty dishes he'd taken from the Captains quarters, spilling everything across the deck.

The day before that, Paublo had seen Diego pin Bo against the hatch wall simply because he was in his path. He had threatened Bo with his dagger.

Through it all Bo never said anything. Paublo did however see the look of hatred in his eyes when the others weren't watching. He worried Bo was going to do something to get himself killed. He did not want that to happen. He liked the old man.

He had warned Bo, explaining to him that he would never get to see his beloved homeland if he gave in to his instincts. He didn't think Bo would ever do anything to jeopardize that. It was what he lived for.

44

Days turned to a week as the ships pushed their way through the ocean toward the promise of unexplored lands. Paublo retained his role as lookout and spent as much time in the barrel as he could. Most days were the same and only water filled his view as he scanned the horizons on all sides of the ship.

He had earned his place in the crew and felt like one of them. He knew with a certainty that this life was what he had been born for.

With those pleasant thoughts swirling in his mind, he lifted his head and scanned the sea again. It seemed the horizon was thicker than when he had last looked. As he stared, the hazy blue line began to rise from the sea slowly taking a solid form. With excitement, Paublo realized he was looking at land. He cupped his hands and shouted to the deck below.

Sailors hurried to the rails and stared ahead, some of them pointing excitedly in the direction of the line on the horizon.

Some of them scrambled up the ropes for a better view. Paublo strained his eyes. It was the first time to see the new land, and he had been the first to spot it. An excitement gripped him. He wished the ship would go faster. They didn't have full sail on so that Captain Antonyo's damaged ship could keep up. It would take longer to get there at this speed. He wondered if the captain was thinking the same.

Below, on the deck, he could see Bo standing near the rail. He was shielding his eyes with his hand, staring into the distance. Paublo knew he was hoping it would be his homeland. He felt bad for him, but he knew he wasn't free to leave even if it were his country. He belonged to Captain Gaspar, and if he tried to run he would be captured or shot. Paublo wondered how it was that one man had the right to own another, simply because of the family he was born into.

He turned and watched the horizon. It was no longer straight. It had bumps and valleys, although it was still so far away it remained a hazy blue. It would still take most of the day to get there. He squinted his eyes as he thought he saw movement. Then two seagulls came into focus and soon came in for a landing on the crossbeam of the forward mast.

45

"Land ahead," came the cry from Paublo in the lookout barrel, high overhead.

Gaspar looked up and then turned to stare over the bow of the ship in the direction Paublo was pointing. A faint blue outline appeared on the distant horizon. A cheer rose from the crew who were spread around the deck and on the sail ropes. Land not only promised fresh water and meat but the thrill of being the first to see it and walk on its shores. It was the ultimate feeling for the explorers, and what drove them to set out on these perilous journeys.

Gaspar turned and looked back over the stern rail at the other two carvels. Antonyo's ship limped along directly astern under partial sail, Miguel's followed some distance behind that. He had positioned them that way once they got underway, following the ceremony to commit Jorge's body to the sea.

As he watched the distant blue line, his mind drifted back to his home on Terceira. He wondered what he would find to bring back to his family, and what land he would be able to lay claim to for King Manuel. He hoped they would find natives on this land. The slave trade was more than lucrative and would provide the necessary funding for this adventure. It would also be fortunate if there were furs and fish in this land as well. The excitement and anticipation of exploration gripped him as he scanned the hazy line that rose above the sea in the distance. With this wind, it would take the rest of the day to reach it. He paced the deck, considering laying on full sail and leaving Miguel to escort Antonyo to shore. Finally rationalizing there was no real advantage to that, he decided to continue as they were.

"We have a welcoming party Cap'n," said Fernam, nodding his head toward the distant shore. Gaspar looked up in time to see two fat seagulls swoop in and land on the crossbeam of the forward sail. With a loud scold, one of them lifted its tail and sprayed the sail.

"I guess the voyage has been christened now," laughed Gaspar.

"Yes, sir, that it has," grinned Fernam.

With one more look at the distant blue haze sitting at the edge of the waterline, Gaspar nodded to Fernam, walked to the stairs, left the deck and returned to his cabin to record the activities of the day.

46

Bo kept returning from the galley to stand at the rail watching as the land began to materialize ahead of the ship. Finally, the hazy blue had turned to browns and greens. The hills and cliffs had formed. Trees were now visible. He was not sure anymore. This land was beginning to look much like the land they had left the day they sailed. This might not yet be his homeland.

"Go tell the Captain we are close," the man at the wheel shouted to him.

Glancing up at the barrel where Paublo was standing erect, his eyes locked on the approaching shoreline, Bo stepped away from the rail and made his way to the entrance beneath the wheel deck.

He stepped through the outer door and knocked on the captain's door.

The loud knock startled Gaspar. The logbook lay open on the table in front of him, the quill dangled loosely from his fingers leaving a tiny pool of ink on the polished wooden surface. He must have dozed he realized as his mind refocused. The knock came again.

"Enter," he ordered.

Bo swung the door open, ducked his head and stepped over the threshold. "Been sent to tell you land is close, Cap'n," he said, with eyes averted.

"Thank you, Bo," said Gaspar, as he returned the quill to its stand. Using a cloth, he blotted the ink spill and then pushed his chair back from the table with a loud scraping noise. Taking the great coat Bo was holding out to him, he shrugged it over his shoulders and followed the black man outside, closing the heavy wooden door behind him.

The land they were approaching was heavily wooded, but the coast was protected by high stony cliffs, or bolder-strewn points. Foaming spray was hurled high into the air as the sea dashed itself against the smooth surface of the cliffs. Gaspar climbed the steps to the wheel deck and stood at the rail watching the new land grow closer. He felt the excitement of seeing this place for the first time, knowing he would probably be the first to stand on these shores. This was why he had left the comforts of the Azores in the first place. Looking around at his men, he could see the same feelings registered in their faces as they stared at the approaching shoreline, and further borne out by their animated conversations.

Turning to his helmsman, he gave the order to alter course and follow the coast southward. Somewhere they would find a sheltered harbour where they could make landfall, hopefully before night which was not far away.

47

Paublo stared at the high cliffs that rose up from the water. They were mostly gray with veins of white weaving their way through them in irregular lines. At some of the most unusual places a single tree jutted out from the sheer rock, having somehow found enough soil to place its roots deep enough to survive. *There is nowhere to land a boat here,* Paublo thought. *It would be dashed to pieces by the waves crashing against the smooth rock face.*

He watched as Captain Gaspar emerged from his quarters behind Bo. The captain climbed the steps to the wheel deck and scanned the shoreline. He gave a command and the ship began to turn and follow the coastline.

"Look for a place to land," he shouted to Paublo.

Paublo was nervous. He did not want to take them to a place where the ship could be damaged on hidden shoals. He strained his eyes ahead, looking for a break in the rocky cliffs. And then he saw it.

"There," he shouted down to the deck, as he pointed to what appeared to be a break in the rocky coastline.

Gaspar went to the starboard rail and watched the shoreline pass. Ahead he could see the break Paublo was pointing to. "Trim the sails," he ordered. Sailors began running up the ropes and out along the crossbeams where they released some of the sails, allowing the speed of the ship to drop off.

Coming around the head of the point, a deep bay opened up before them. Paublo could see a beach at the end of the bay. "There's a beach, Captain," he shouted. "We can land there."

In the distance Gaspar could see thick blanketing forest growing almost to the water's edge where a rocky beach ringed the inner harbour. A narrow stream spilled into the bay on the far left, nestled in the shadow of a tall cliff.

More sails were dropped, and the ship's forward speed fell off quickly to a slow drift while sailors at the bow sounded the bottom as they approached the beach.

"Getting shallow here, Captain," shouted the sailor who was doing the sounding.

"Stop her here," ordered Gaspar. The rattling of the rusty anchor chain broke the stillness of the sheltered harbour, and the ship came to a stop as the heavy anchor bit into the seabed. Chains rattled as the other two ships dropped anchor nearby.

Boats were launched over the side of each ship and rowed to the shore. Gaspar stood in the stern of his, surveying the country. Behind him the moon had appeared over the edge of the sea, sending a glittering silver trail across the quiet water. In its illumination Gaspar could see the outline of tall trees running back for some distance from the shoreline where they followed the slope up to the top of a large flat hill. He determined to make his way up there tomorrow to get a better look at the land.

The bow of the boat ground on the pebbly bottom and the sailors shipped their oars and jumped into the shallow water. They pulled the boat onto the beach and Gaspar placed his hand on the gunwale and jumped over the side onto the loose beach rocks.

Accompanied by Pedro and Diego who were carrying their guns, Gaspar walked up the beach to the edge of the surrounding forest and stuck the Portuguese flag he carried into the soft sod. "I herby claim this land for King Manuel and Portugal," he said.

There was no record that he was aware of that previous explorers had come this far south. This was new land he had discovered. He decided he would explore its length before returning home to Portugal.

The men set about cutting trees to build temporary shelters while the row boats ferried more men and supplies from the three ships. It would take some time to make the repairs on

Antonyo's ship. Gaspar expected this would be their home for a week or two. He walked back to a rowboat that was unloading water barrels to be refilled with fresh water at the stream at the far end of the beach.

He was rowed back to the ship in the empty rowboat. Lanterns had been lit and placed around the rails. Their reflection danced on the gently moving water. *This is a peaceful place*, he thought. He wondered if there were natives in the forest, and if they were watching the activity.

As he climbed the rope ladder, the soft twitter of night birds was the only sound not made by the work his men were doing on the beach.

48

Today Paublo was going ashore. He had been told to stay on the ship yesterday. He and Bo had stood at the rail and watched the row boats ferrying supplies to the beach from the three ships and the setup of the temporary camp as the night set in.

An early morning mist lay over the harbour, partially obscuring the shore. The noise of the crews on the beach was muted by its heavy blanket.

Captain Antonyo's ship had been beached in the early morning and tilted on its side to allow the men to begin the repairs. Only its masts were visible over the swirling cloud.

While all this was going on, Paublo had climbed the rigging to his barrel to see the country. From here he could see over the low mist and it gave him a much better vantage point, but he couldn't see over the hill that stood behind the beach. He did see what seemed like smoke far off in the distance, but he couldn't be sure. He wondered if it might be the campfires of natives. He decided not to tell anyone. He couldn't be sure of what he was seeing, and he figured they would soon find out anyway. He had heard Captain Gaspar was planning to scout the countryside. If there was smoke, he would discover it then.

As he watched, the light breeze from the ocean whisked away the mist, revealing the beach with Captain Antonyo's ship partially out of the water, lying on its side. Around it the sailors were busy working on the damage. A number of shelters had been built along the edge of the forest and the setup of the camp was well underway.

Below, a rowboat was pushing off from the ship, carrying Captain Gaspar and Captain Miguel as well as Alfonso and Diego who were carrying their long guns.

They beached the boat, collected their things and walked up the loose stones into the woods near where the Portuguese flag fluttered in the wind.

Paublo climbed down to the deck to meet the returning rowboat. He tried to suppress his excitement but couldn't help grinning at Bo who was bringing food from the galley to be taken ashore. Bo smiled back. He too was anxious to stand on this new land. It wasn't his home country, but maybe it was closer to it.

Once all the food was loaded, Paublo joined Bo in the boat and they were taken to the beach. Paublo leaned on the gunwale and dragged his hand in the water. Beneath the surface he could see fish swimming near the shell-littered bottom.

The boat bumped the loose beach rock and he leaped over the side into the shallow water and waded ashore. This was the first new land he had ever had a chance to stand on. This made up for what he had to go through in the storm. This made him an explorer like Captain Gaspar.

Bending down, he selected a small beach rock with an irregular white line weaving through its smooth grey surface. He turned it over in his fingers thinking no one had ever touched it before. *This is what exploring is all about, being the first,* he thought. He slipped the stone into his pocket. He would give it to Maria when he returned home. Feeling a little guilty, he selected another for his mother.

He glanced over his shoulder. Bo was watching him curiously, a half smile on his dark face.

"Let's get this unloaded," said one of the rowers sharply. "There's a lot of mouths to feed. No time for idleness."

49

The days had passed without incident since the camp had been built in a clearing at the edge of the river, a short distance from the coast. Old mamateeks had been repaired and new ones built. There had been no sign of any Shannok, and the band had settled into a daily routine they were familiar with. During the days the work kept them busy and, in the evenings, they enjoyed time together around the campfires, sharing stories of the day and of days past. Repeating the stories of their ancestors ensured the history of their people would be remembered and passed along to their children.

The drying racks were spread with fish from both the river and the sea. Shellfish and bird's eggs were being cooked and ground into powder for storage for the long snow season. The skins of smaller animals were stretched on racks around the busy camp. Small children ran and played around the clearing, and women chatted happily as they worked. Crows and seagulls had found the camp and fought each other for the tasty morsels discarded around the clearing, adding to the everyday noise.

Soon it would be time to hunt the caribou. Some of the men had been busy knocking down trees to build the run that would guide the caribou into the river where they could be harvested. Daygon was happy with the way things were going. *We will be well prepared for the snow season this year*, he thought.

Standing just outside the open door of his mamateek, he smiled as he surveyed the activity in the clearing, letting the sounds of the playing children, conversations of the women, and singing of one of the men working on a tapaithook (canoe) fill his head. Everything was as it should be, just as it had been every year before. He was happy for his band. He just wished it hadn't been marred by the incident with the Shannok.

Today he was going to help with the caribou run. He picked up his Dthoonanven (stone axe) and slid it into the loop in his belt. With a wave to Shandowee and Gadedoo he turned and followed the men into the woods.

50

In the morning Gaspar was joined by Miguel in his quarters where they had breakfast together.

"What is your plan, Gaspar?" asked Miguel, as they sat back in their chairs with steaming cups of coffee in their hands, after Bo had left with the breakfast dishes.

"What do you think of him?" asked Gaspar, motioning toward the door.

"Who? Bo?"

"Yes, Bo."

"Harmless. A good slave."

"I'm not sure. Sometimes I get a feeling there's a suppressed rage in him."

"Never noticed anything myself."

"Something in his eyes sometimes makes me wonder."

"Well, just keep a close eye on him and use the whip if he gets out of line."

"That's what I've been thinking."

"So, what's your plan?"

"Today the men will beach Antonyo's ship to allow the repairs to the mast and rails. Antonyo will be taking a crew to search for a suitable tree for the mast, and the rest of the men will complete temporary shelters. I thought you and I could hike to the top of the ridge and look at the country."

"Guess we will be here for a while, so we might as well do some hunting. There should be plenty of animals in these thick woods."

"That stream should provide a good fresh water supply. Some of our barrels were refilled there last night.

"I thought I would send a crew out to the mouth of the harbour to try for fish," said Miguel.

"Good idea."

"This place looks much more habitable than the land we encountered on last years voyage."

"It is and I expect it will get better the further south we go."

"I agree. We will find out once the ships are repaired. Let's get ashore and do some exploring, brother."

171

Gaspar set the empty cup down, pushed back the chair and stood to his feet. He picked up a cutlass and strapped it on, handed Miguel a musket and they walked out onto the deck. They climbed down the ladder, boarded Miguel's rowboat and were taken to shore.

Already the beach was a hive of activity. Antonyo had his crew busy working on his beached ship. Several small shelters were finished or being worked on at the edge of the beach.

Antonyo was in the process of assembling a five-man crew to help him find a suitable tree for the new mast.

"We are going to the top of the ridge to scout the country," said Gaspar. "We will take two of the soldiers with us in case we run into unfriendly natives."

Antonyo grinned at him. "Bring them back," he said. "We could use the help."

Accompanied by Alfonso and Diego, two of the soldiers from his own crew, Gaspar led the small party into the thick woods that ringed the beach. After ten minutes of navigating through the heavier forest they found a small stream that wound its way through the undergrowth in search of a path to the sea. The men drank their fill of the cool refreshing water and then pushed on toward the higher ground they had spotted when on the beach. The slope gradually increased and at places larger boulders and loose rock forced them to search for easier paths.

It was at one of those places where the others were alerted by a cry from Miguel who had gone in search of a better path. "Over here," he shouted, "Come see this."

When Gaspar and the other two reached him, he was standing and pointing at the soft ground. The outline of a bare adult foot was clearly visible in the damp mud.

"Native," said Alfonso, as he unslung his long gun from his shoulder and dropped powder and shot from the bag at his side into the long muzzle. He tamped it home with the rod and lifted it to his shoulder as he scanned the surrounding woods.

"Keep an eye on the woods, but don't fire unless we are threatened," commanded Gaspar, peering around.

"Here's another one," said Diego, pointing at the ground. "It looks like they are following this path. It seems to be leading up to the top of the ridge."

"We will follow it then," Gaspar announced. "These prints are not old. Someone was probably watching the activity on the beach. If there is one there are more."

As they neared the top of the hill the trees thinned out, and the crest was only covered in low brush and clumps of thick berry bushes surrounding the jagged granite that pushed through the surface here and there.

Standing on the crest, they could see the path they were following meander down the other side of the hill and disappear into the woods. In the distance was the dark water of a small lake with native teepees dotting its shores. Columns of smoke drifted lazily into the sky and people could be seen moving around the village. Two canoes were being paddled across the lake.

Gaspar looked at Miguel. "This voyage might pay off after all," he said with a grin. "Looks as if there might be a fair number of them."

Miguel nodded in agreement. He looked back at the activity on the beach. "When should we go in there? There's still plenty of work to do on Antonyo's ship. We've probably got a week or so."

"Once they discover us there's a risk of scaring them off. We could store them below deck on your boat until the others are done," said Gaspar.

"We have no idea if they are friendly or hostile."

"They most likely have never seen a white man before, so we should be prepared for anything. Let's get back to the beach. We'll do an early morning raid. That's probably the best time to surprise them."

51

Paublo and Bo were standing by the rail watching the sun slip beneath the water when the scouting group returned, discussing the sighting of a native camp and the plans for a raiding party in the morning. He saw the slump in Bo's shoulders when he heard the conversation. He knew it brought back all the nightmarish memories of his capture.

Paublo watched as Bo backed away from the rail and averted his eyes when Diego climbed the rope ladder ahead of Gaspar.

"Get me some supper, Bo," the captain ordered. Bo turned and hurried to the hatch and disappeared through the door.

Standing by the rail, Paublo turned Maria's stone over and over in his pocket. It felt like a connection to her somehow. He imagined how much she would enjoy being here to see all this. With a sigh he looked up at the starlit sky that he knew hung over both of them and made his way to the hatch and then down the two flights of stairs to the crew quarters. Most of the men were ashore and he had the room mostly to himself. As he lay in his hammock in the near darkness, he wrapped his hand tightly around the stone. It was not only a link to Maria, but also his link to this new land. As long as he had it, it would be a reminder of his first voyage.

It was taking longer to fall asleep than usual. He realized he missed the constant motion of the ship. He wondered if that made him a sailor. He decided it did. He wondered how he would get to sleep when he was back on dry land. He thought he probably wouldn't be spending a lot of time there anyway.

52

That night, as he was drifting to sleep to the soft gurgling sounds of the nearby river, the quiet murmuring of night birds, and the gentle whistle of the wind passing over the smoke hole at the top of the mamateek, Shandowee reached out in the darkness, gently took his hand and placed it on her belly.

"Is it true?" he asked sleepily.

"Yes, my husband. Gadedoo is going to have a little sister or a little brother."

Wrapping his arms around her, Daygon kissed her tenderly on the cheek. "You have made me very happy, Shandowee," he whispered. "Maybe it will be a little girl. That would make our family complete."

"I am glad you are happy. I am too."

"I love you, Shandowee," murmured Daygon, as he drifted off to sleep with a wide smile on his face, visions of a little girl asleep on his shoulder already invading his dreams.

The next morning as he carved meat from the caribou he'd hung from the tree just outside his mamateek door, he discovered the smile still lingered. There was a new joy in his heart, the work was easier, his mind was occupied with thoughts of the new baby. When Bragadessh spoke behind him he jumped in surprise, the blade of the knife nicking his finger, bringing a bead of blood to the surface. He raised his finger to his lips and licked the blood away.

"Where is your mind today?" asked Bragadessh with a smile.

With an even wider grin, Daygon replied, "I have news, brother. Good news."

"What news could make you so happy?"

"Shandowee is going to have a baby."

"That is good news, Daygon", said Bragadessh, as he wrapped his arms around his brother and gave him a bearhug.

"What will you call him?" he said, pushing him back to arms length.

"Her."

"Then, what will you call her?" laughed Bragadessh. "And how do you know this?"

"I just know. I have to think some more about her name."

53

A continuous tapping pulled Gaspar back from his dream. He had been running with his brothers and sisters through the green fields of Terceira, a lively game of tag the only thing on their minds. Opening his eyes, he realized the tapping was the sound of rain beating on the other side of the thick plank walls of his quarters. He immediately thought of the planned trek through the wet woods to the native camp, and considered postponing it. Then he reasoned the rain might be an advantage. The natives would probably stay in their teepees on a day like this, making it much easier to round them up.

He was dressing when Cook knocked on the door with his breakfast. "Looks to be a wet day, Captain," he said, as he ducked his head and stepped over the threshold, dripping water on the polished plank floor. "'Spect 'twas the rolls of thunder that woke you up, sir," he said, as another crash of thunder boomed and rolled away into the distance.

Gaspar slipped his shirt over his head and sat at the table as Cook laid out the hot breakfast. "Where's Bo this morning?" he asked.

"Busy in the galley, sir. Thought I'd bring breakfast myself, since we are no longer at sea."

"Are the crews on the beach yet?" he asked.

"Yes, sir, they are. Busy taking out that broken mast from Captain Antonyo's ship. 'Spect they'll have it replaced in two or maybe three days."

"That'll be good, Cook. We are just wasting time here. It's time we moved on."

"New places to discover," said Cook with a grin, as he stepped out the door into the rain.

Gaspar dipped the end of the piece of bread into the broken yolks of the three steaming eggs staring up at him from his plate, and then stuffed it in his mouth, following it up with hot coffee. Swallowing the food, he savored the little pleasure for a moment, then hurried through what remained on his plate. He was anxious to get ashore and make the trek through the woods to the native camp.

Pushing back his chair, he stood to his feet, swung his heavy cape over his shoulders, pulled a leather cap on his head and stepped outside.

54

The heavy plank door squeaked open on its iron hinges, letting outside light into the stuffy room. Blinking awake he raised himself up on one elbow causing the hammock to swing gently. Francisco was standing between the hammocks dripping water unto the spreading pool on the deck planks beneath his feet.

"Heavy rain out there this morning, son," he said. "Best dress for it or you'll be soaked soon as you get on deck."

Paublo unfolded his cramped hand that was still tightly gripping Maria's stone. He wriggled his fingers to get rid of the stiffness, then swung his feet to the floor and slipped them into his boots. He picked the stone from the hammock, looked at it for a moment, dropped it into his pocket and then followed Francisco up the stairs.

He was remembering bits of last night's dream. He had been back in Terceira with Maria at the fish stand, reliving the first time he met her.

55

As he stepped onto the deck, Gaspar hunched his shoulders against the heavy rain and called to Pedro, Diego and Afonso. "Get your weapons and come with me to shore. We are going slave hunting today. Take some extra guns for the sailors who will be joining us to help round up the natives."

The three men went below and reappeared a few minutes later with several guns and canisters of powder which they lowered to the sailors in the waiting rowboat.

Gaspar followed them over the side and down the rope ladder into the gently rocking boat.

Paublo stepped out of the hatch door into a downpour of rain and was soaked before he reached the rail where the raiding party was climbing down into the rowboat. One of the rowers motioned him to join them and he scrambled down the slippery rope ladder and found a seat between two of the soldiers. They were trying to shield their gun powder to keep it dry. Paublo was huddled forward doing his best to keep the cold rain from getting inside his shirt and running down his back.

He looked up to see the captain was watching him. "You're coming with us today," Gaspar said. "We are going to raid the village we saw from the hilltop yesterday. We should capture us some slaves before the day is done. You've earned a spot on the raiding party, son."

"Thank you, sir," Paublo said, and dropped his eyes to the floor of the boat. A flurry of emotions swirled through his head. He was happy the captain wanted to include him because that meant he was seeing him as a sailor, but he was not comfortable capturing natives and enslaving them. He couldn't get Bo's story out of his mind and he didn't want to be a part of something that did that to someone else.

"Wet day for the powder, sir," said Diego. "Might be tricky to get the muskets to fire."

Looking up at the sky, Gaspar replied, "Looks like it might clear up soon. The sky is brighter over there. Keep your powder dry for now. Chances are we won't need it anyway. Hopefully we'll catch them by surprise."

"Probably a good chance in this rain sir."

They were nearing the beach when Afonso, the soldier sitting on his right, suddenly jumped to his feet and pointed excitedly. "What's going on over there?" he asked loudly.

Gaspar turned and looked in the direction he was pointing.

Paublo grabbed the seat with both hands to steady himself from the sudden rocking of the boat and craned around Afonso to see what he was pointing at.

Down at the far end of the beach a large group of natives had emerged from the woods at the base of the cliff that rose some twenty feet into the air above the stream that flowed into the bay. Some were seating themselves on the loose beach rock, others remained standing and were talking excitedly as they pointed to the ship laying on its side at the edge of the water.

The group contained men, women and children. Some of them were dressed in tunics that hung below their knees, some were bare chested with leggings. Most of them wore long braids, some tipped with bird feathers. Several of the men carried long bows that were taller than they were, others carried spears. Everything they wore and carried seemed to be dyed red.

The ones that seemed to be women carried furs from a variety of animals in bundles on their back.

The men on the beach and around Antonyo's ship had stopped their activity and stood staring down at the end of the cove. Those with guns picked them up. Others pulled their cutlasses from their belts.

"Wait," shouted Gaspar, as his boat ground its keel on the beach. He stood and jumped over the side. He had noticed some of the Indians had bows strapped to their backs, but none were held in their hands. "They look friendly," he continued, as he strode up the beach to where the sailors had gathered.

Paublo heard the Captain's words. He had also been wondering if the natives were dangerous. He stayed seated as the others jumped out and pulled the boat ashore. Looking down the cove, he watched the children amongst the natives. Most of them were standing at the edge of the woods behind the adults. Some of them were talking and pointing excitedly at the men and big ship on the beach. None of them wore any clothes over their red bodies. The rain did not seem to bother any of them.

Glancing back at the ship, he saw Bo leaning on the rail watching. He wondered what he was thinking. He thought he knew.

"Get some of the trinkets in the hold of Antonyo's ship. We might be able to do this more peacefully," ordered Gaspar.

To Miguel, who had joined him, he said, "If we can get their trust now, we won't have to take them until the repairs are done. Then we won't have to waste men on guard duty to protect us from any reprisals."

"Look, two of them are coming this way," said Miguel.

Gaspar waited as the two natives slowly approached and stopped a short distance from where they were standing. One of them lifted the two furs he was carrying on his shoulder and let them fall to the ground. He picked up one and held it out. It looked like a red fox. Rainwater dripped from the end of its snout onto the stones at his feet.

Gaspar glanced at Miguel and stepped forward. The Indian was dressed in an animal-skin cloak worn with the fur inside, draped over his shoulders, hanging to his knees. A beaver skin was attached at the top and served as a collar. His bare arms, legs and face were all painted red, as was the cloak. His long black hair hung in a braid down his back, with a black feather protruding from the crown. His weather-creased face was hairless.

Gaspar looked up from the native's bare feet to find his face split in a wide grin, his dark eyes twinkling. He pushed the fur toward Gaspar and spoke some gibberish, ending with a short laugh.

Gaspar accepted the fur. It was soft to the touch. He ran his hand down the length, closing his hand around the thick tail. *This will fetch a fine price in Portugal*, he thought. *I wonder if they have more.* Turning, he waved for the sailor whom he had dispatched for the trinkets to join him.

Reaching into the cloth bag, he drew out a handful of colored beads and a small handheld mirror. He held them out to the native.

The native accepted them with a gleeful smile and waved for Gaspar to follow him as he turned and, with his companion, quickly made his way across the wet stones toward where the other natives had gathered.

Gaspar looked at Miguel, raised his eyebrows and followed. "This might be easier than we thought," he said. "They don't seem afraid of us."

"Should save us from hiking through the wet woods," replied Miguel, with a laugh.

The two natives ahead of them stopped, turned and joined the laughter, and then continued walking toward their waiting companions.

When Gaspar and Miguel reached the group, their leader had already shown them the colored beads and they were examining them excitedly, exclaiming in their peculiar language as they each got to hold them in their hands.

Others were competing like children to see themselves in the little mirror, uttering squeals of delight as their images stared back at them.

Animal skins were spread on the ground, piled with dried meat and fish. It was obvious to Gaspar they had come to trade.

Paublo stood on the beach near the rowboat and watched.

56

The nightmares pushed their way into Bo's dreams that night. Kelanti was there. The white men were attacking their village. Black men from some other tribe were helping them. The villagers were screaming and running in panic. They had all heard of these white men who took people. They knew the people never came back.

He tried to shout a warning as Kelanti began to run. One of the white men was chasing him, swinging a large club over his head. Bo tried to run to help his grandson, but his feet were heavy. He struggled to lift them for each agonizing step, but he could see the white man was gaining. He watched in horror as the club began an arc that would bring it down on Kelanti. He screamed a warning and came fully awake. He was soaked in sweat and his body was shaking. He shook his head to rid himself of the terrifying pictures.

He had stayed awake the rest of the night, only venturing inside the hatch when the rain started. He had returned outside when the first light had announced the new day.

Standing at the rail, he watched the raiding party and the boy leave the ship for the beach. They were almost there when he saw the natives emerge from the woods. It looked like the whole village was there, from the smallest child to the oldest man.

These were the people the raiding party had hoped to capture, and now they had come to them. He wished he had some way to warn them of the fate they faced, but he knew he was helpless to do anything.

Their excitement over the colored beads and mirrors told him they had never seen white men before. They had no idea what was coming.

He turned away and made his way down to the galley.

57

The natives stayed, building temporary shelters at the end of the beach. They could be seen watching curiously as the repairs progressed on Antonyo's ship. It had become their pastime as they gathered each morning and sat around their campfires at the edge of the beach, discussing the activity going on around the beached ship.

Paublo watched them from a distance. He was haunted by the stories Bo had told him, knowing a similar fate awaited the unsuspecting natives. Yet he felt he owed his loyalty to Captain Gaspar for agreeing to bring him on this voyage. He wished Maria was here to talk to. He wondered what she would tell him to do.

The more he thought about it, the more he realized there was nothing he could do anyway. He just had to watch all this unfold, no matter how much he disliked it. He decided he would spend the most of his time on the ship and not on the beach.

On the second day, he watched from his high perch as the natives cooked a caribou on an open fire. When the sun was high overhead, they carved up the meat and brought it on large slabs of birch rind to the men working on Captain Antonyo's ship.

Work stopped for some time as both the natives and sailors feasted together. Paublo watched as the two groups seemed to communicate without speaking as they shared the meal together. Looking at the scene from this distance it almost seemed they were friends. He expected the natives felt that way too.

58

It was several days later before the new mast was seated and secured and the work to attach the yardarms and the rigging began. The new mast was neither the length nor the quality of the old one, but was the best they could find in the nearby woods. Gaspar and Antonyo felt it would get them back to the Azores where a proper one could be installed, even though it would most likely take longer to get there.

That evening, the three captains gathered in Gaspar's quarters. Cook and Bo brought them dishes of baked cod and an assortment of shellfish, all gathered from the sea around them. The warm smells of cooked fish filled the crowded room, reminding each of them of how long it had been since they had eaten this well.

After the feast was over, the chairs were pushed back and talk soon turned to the voyage.

"We should be ready to get underway in a couple of days," said Antonyo, contentedly picking seafood from his teeth as he leaned back in his chair until it rested against the cabin wall.

"The repairs are progressing well," remarked Miguel.

"How do you think she'll behave with that new mast?" asked Gaspar.

"I think it will be fine, probably much less maneuverable and a lot slower, but manageable."

"I think there are enough natives here to fill your ships," said Gaspar. "That, along with the abundance of fish, should more than pay for the voyage."

"And give us a tidy profit as well," said Miguel, with a grin.

"That it should," said Antonyo.

"With a load and that short mast, I think you and Miguel should return to Terceira. There is no reason for you to continue on."

"Makes sense. What will you do?"

"I will continue south for a few more days, scout the land and round up another load of natives."

"It would be good to find out how big this place is," said Miguel. "King Manuel would want to know the extent of the land we have claimed for him."

"It is decided then," said Gaspar pushing back his chair and standing. Miguel and Antonyo followed suit and stepped out the door.

Gaspar returned to his chair and sat quietly, listening to the sounds from the nearby beach coming through the partially open porthole at the back of the room. He could hear faint singing from the direction of the native camp.

59

Paublo had watched the Indians move closer to Antonyo's ship as the days went on, their curiosity getting the better of them. Now they congregated on the beach at the edge of the woods directly above the beached ship. The bolder children ran and played where the men were working, often gathering around the fire pit where Cook prepared the meals for those ashore. Cook sometimes made a game of tossing scraps and watching them fight each other for each morsel. It reminded Paublo of the seagulls. It was not as entertaining for him as it was for some of the other sailors.

Yesterday, the work on the mast had been completed and the ship righted and propped up on sticks wedged under the gunwales. Today it would be refloated at high tide.

Standing near the ship, Antonyo waved to the natives, beckoning them to come to where he was. Two of the men approached Antonyo, haltingly at first, unsure of what the white man wanted. Once they reached him and the others saw nothing happened, five more left the group and joined them.

They are just like children, thought Paublo.

Captain Antonyo turned and climbed up to the deck on the wooden ladder propped against the side of the ship. Standing on the deck with a broad inviting smile, he motioned them to follow. This sparked an animated conversation amongst the seven natives. Eventually it seemed they convinced themselves it was safe, and they followed each other up the ladder, all but one. He walked away and returned to the watching group.

From his high vantage point Paublo could see Captain Antonyo lead the men around the deck, touching the gear strewn around the ship in wonder as they passed. They talked animatedly and gestured to each other as each new item came within their reach. The natives were clearly awed by the size of everything, touching the ropes, the ships wheel and the giant mast, exclaiming excitedly to each other as they craned their necks back to see the wrapped sails high overhead.

Paublo had overheard the captains talking last night about the benefit of showing the natives around the ship with the expectation it would make it easier to get them aboard when it was refloated. He knew it was a trick. Part of him still wished he could warn them.

As Antonyo led them down through the open hatchway and down the stairs below the deck they became more subdued. He noticed some were glancing anxiously back the way they had come. He stepped into the candle lit galley where he had arranged a trunk be left open with trinkets and colored cloth. Pointing to it, he indicated the men should help themselves.

Each in turn selected something and left the rest. Antonyo wondered at their restraint. He wouldn't have expected his sailors to have acted that way.

Returning to the top deck, the natives began talking amongst themselves again. It was clear the time below deck had made them feel uncomfortable. They clambered down the ladder to the beach and quickly walked away in the direction of their camp.

After they left, the crews set about preparing the ship for launch at high tide. By noon everything from the beach had been ferried back to the other two waiting ships and the six rowboats returned for the unsuspecting natives.

Soon, the tide began to creep up the beach underneath the stern of the ship. The sailors began to roll the boat down the beach on logs that had been placed underneath it. Natives from the group joined in and pushed side by side with the sailors. When the ship slid into the water it pushed a large wave behind it and floated free, only attached to the land by a long rope. A cheer arose from the sailors, immediately joined by the whole native band that had gathered on the beach to watch the proceedings.

Antonyo searched the crowd and found the men he had previously taken aboard his ship, and with much encouragement coaxed them into his rowboat. As they pushed away from the shore, lines began to form to the remaining boats, and they began to fill with natives who wanted to get their own view of the big ships. There was a visible excitement rippling through the crowd at the chance to get aboard one of the ships as the first group had earlier in the day, and to see what they had seen.

The soldiers standing at the end of the line turned away women and children, ensuring only men and older boys were allowed in the boats. The women and children gathered in a group on the beach waiting their turn and watched as their husbands, fathers and sons were rowed out to Antonyo and Miguel's ships.

Once all the natives were on the decks, the rowboats were swung aboard. Sailors ran up the riggings, out on the crossbeams, and unfurled the sails. The anchors were pulled aboard, and the ships began to move out of the harbour. Using swords, whips and spears, the crew herded the natives below deck, where they were chained together, lying flat on their backs on stacked wooden shelves, amid shouts of surprise and anger.

Those left on the beach heard the cries of alarm and were screaming in fear as they finally realized what was happening, powerless to do anything about it. Some of them ran along the water's edge, crying out to their companions as the ships sailed away.

From his perch, Paublo watched the distraught natives running along the beach in despair. He saw one mother fall to her knees and gather two children to her. He knew this was wrong. Looking down at the deck, he saw Bo standing at the rail staring at the receding beach, his shoulders hunched and his head down. He suspected he knew the kind of sadness that Bo was feeling and the memories this must be stirring in him. He felt sorry for him.

60

Gaspar pulled anchor and followed the other two ships out of the harbour. He felt pleased. Between the two ships they had a total of fifty-seven slaves. It made for crowded quarters, but the crossing would be about a month, even with the makeshift mast on Antonyo's ship. The natives should all survive that.

These slaves would more than pay for the voyage. Any additional natives he captured would be purely profit, and this place promised to have plenty of them.

Outside the harbour, Gaspar hove to and watched as his brother and Antonyo set sail in the direction of home. As the ships grew smaller with distance, he ordered the remaining sails up and got underway, following the coastline into uncharted waters. The feeling that he was the first to see this land was the thrill that he had hoped for when he left Terceira, and as he watched the wooded coastline slide by on the starboard side, the feeling of adventure was strong. This was the only place he wanted to be, and in a way, he was glad to be alone.

They had already accomplished much, but he knew there was much more to see in this place. He felt his discovery would secure his place in history, but he was not done yet.

61

Life at the coastal camp had settled into a peaceful and familiar routine. There had been no sign of the Shannok. The danger had passed, and the band no longer lived in a constant state of readiness. The days were spent gathering food and preparing it to store for the season of snow. Everyone was busy doing something to help. Even the children had small tasks to do.

The snow season had ravaged the tapaithooks that had been left behind the previous year, so two new ones had been built from the rind stripped from large birch trees surrounding the camp. Earlier this morning, Daygon and three other men had taken the two tapaithooks down river through the mist and paddled out the bay to a nearby island where they planned to gather shellfish.

The morning had gone well. The baskets were full. The men sat around a small fire preparing some of the shellfish for lunch. Daygon sat watching the green shell of the heavy clawed fish turn red as the heat of the fire cooked the juicy meat inside. He licked his lips in anticipation. It had been a long time since he had tasted its tender meat. These four had made the mistake of hiding under a rock too close to shore.

Using a stick, he hooked one from the fire and cracked the shell with a rock. The warm meat was as good as he remembered. He ate slowly, savoring the meal, occasionally wiping away the trickle of juice from the corner of his mouth with the back of his hand. *The warm season is much better than the snow season*, he thought.

He looked around the fire at his companions; Pugathoite, who had fought the Shannok with him, and the two brothers, Grodelle and Sholammette. He had known them all since he was a boy. They had grown up together and shared many adventures, some of them imagined, some of them real. It was good to spend time together like this, not having to worry about the Shannok or the responsibilities of the band, just to enjoy the day.

By the time they were finished, the sun, occasionally hidden by the passing clouds, had reached the top of its journey and had begun its slow slide down the other side. The beach around them was littered with discarded shells.

Daygon stood to his feet, stretched expansively, kicked sand over the embers of fire and said, "It's time to get back to camp. The women will want to cook these before dark," indicating the baskets of shellfish sitting next to the upended tapaithooks.

The men pushed to their feet, gathered up their belongings and walked down the beach to the water's edge. With a man on each end, they lifted the tapaithooks and walked them into the water, loaded the baskets and their weapons, scrambled aboard, and began to paddle out of the little sheltered cove into the open water of the bay.

Daygon glanced back over his shoulder. Crows had already found the remains of their feast and were rooting around the broken shells next to a wispy trail of smoke drifting into the air. He smiled contentedly and dipped his paddle.

As they rounded the point, Pugathoite, who was paddling at the front of Daygon's tapaithook, exclaimed in alarm, "What is that?"

There in the distance, close to the shore where the river emptied into the sea, was a giant boat with enormous white sails. Tiny figures could be seen walking on the high wooden decks and in the air amongst the sails. The four Beothuk sat there in their bobbing tapaithooks with their paddles resting on their knees staring in amazement. They had never seen a boat so big.

Suddenly Daygon broke the spell. "They are going into the river," he shouted in alarm. "They will find our camp. They may be dangerous. We have to get back there." The peace he had been feeling turned to fear, a cold dread that their world was about to be threatened again. This time it might be from an unknown enemy that might be too powerful to fight. He was suddenly scared for the band.

In unison, the four dug their paddles deep into the water and began to pull toward the boat that was disappearing around the first bend in the river. Only the higher sails were visible over the trees.

Daygon's mind was filled with uneasiness. He suspected there were a lot of men on a boat that big. He had no way to warn the band. The muscles in his shoulders bulged as he dipped his paddle deeper and pulled with all the strength he could muster.

62

The days were getting warmer. The wind blowing from the south chased away the last of the winter chill. The heavier coats and capes were discarded, replaced with lighter tunics. The change seemed to have an effect on the sailor's spirits as well. There was more singing and whistling as they worked. The ship was filled with an air of anticipation as they sailed along the coast. It had been almost a week since they parted ways with the other ships.

Paublo spent as much time as he could in the barrel. The view was so much better. He thought about home as he watched the shoreline slip by. He would be working in the fields now if he were back there. This was better, a lot better, even if Maria wasn't here, he thought a little guiltily. He returned to whistling as well.

He saw a large dark shape pass under the ship then surface on the other side and burst out of the water with a mighty splash. It was the first whale he had seen. Its huge fan tail slapped down on the water with a crack, sending spray over the rail.

Seagulls flocked around the spot where the whale went down, searching for any floating morsel left behind as it dove through swarms of smaller fish.

When the gulls weren't chasing the big fish for a free meal they were perched on the mast and sails of the ship, often times near his barrel, the younger ones still covered in their coats of dark feathers. They had little fear.

The coastline was changing too. The jagged cliffs they had encountered in the first weeks, had given way to thickly carpeted rolling hills, gently sloping down to rock-covered beaches.

From his high vantage point he had also spotted herds of large animals on the bogs back from the coast. He suspected they were caribou, like the one the natives had cooked for the sailors. There seemed to be more than he could count.

63

Gaspar had not slept late since they parted company with his brother and Antonyo. The early dawn of each morning found him on the wheel deck watching the changing coastline slowly pass by. He did not want to miss any of this new land. Each night he would update his journal with sketches of the coast and detailed descriptions of what he had seen. He believed he was the first to capture this and it gave him great satisfaction to know he was sailing where no one had sailed before, not even his father.

He wanted to find a place that would take them further into the interior before making landfall again. Just before noon he saw a what he thought looked promising. As they rounded a heavily wooded point, the coastline opened into what appeared to be a large bay. Gaspar ordered the ship turned and entered the bay, passing several large, tree covered islands as they sailed along. None of them showed any signs of being inhabited.

It wasn't till noon that they reached the entrance to a wide river that emptied into the bay.

The sails were trimmed, and they slowly sailed up the middle of the river. A sailor was stationed at the bow to sound the river depth as they went. The riverbanks on both sides were covered with tall birch trees, their leaves only now beginning to open on the large branches that overhung the water.

Standing in the shallow water near the far bank, two caribou raised their heads from the water they were drinking to watch the strange boat move upriver.

"Should we get them, sir?" shouted one of the sailors.

"No," Gaspar replied. "There'll be more upriver."

"Looks like we might not be alone, Cap'n," said Fernam, pointing over the starboard bow. "That's smoke up there."

"More natives I expect," said Gaspar.

Just ahead, the river made a sharp bend and the ship began to slow as the current pushed back against it. Gaspar ordered a little more sail and the ship responded as the wind filled the canvass and pushed them forward.

Moments later, a shout came from Paublo in his lookout barrel, "Natives ahead on the starboard side, Captain."

Gaspar stepped to the rail and watched the shoreline as the ship slowly rounded the bend. The edge of the river was dotted with teepees, smoke drifting from the top of most of them. The natives were lining the river's edge, some pointing excitedly at the large ship as it approached.

Noticing some of the native men were standing protectively in front of the others with their bows drawn, Gaspar ordered his soldiers to make their muskets ready.

"Anchor away," ordered Gaspar as the ship drew abreast of the camp.

The anchor chain rattled over the side and dropped into the water.

Sailors clambered up the ropes and dropped the sails and the river tide turned the ship and pulled it downstream until the anchor chain came taut, bringing it to a stop.

"What's your plan, sir?" asked Diego.

"We'll take the two rowboats and go ashore. Load up some of the trinkets. Give everyone a gun but no shooting unless we are fired upon by them," he said, indicating the men with drawn bows. "Ten men to a boat."

Diego and Alfonso organized the men and passed out the guns while the boats were being lowered into the water.

"Keep your guns down," ordered Gaspar from the lead boat. "Let's not do anything to alarm them. We don't want to have to shoot any of the men. The more of them we can capture the better."

211

The natives backed away from the shore as the two boats reached the riverbank.

Gaspar opened the neck of the bag of trinkets and tossed it toward the group, spilling colored beads and silver hand mirrors on the ground. At first the natives stood there looking at the shiny objects, until one of the young children broke away from the crowd and ran to the bag. Dipping his hands into the contents he filled them and lifted them in the air letting the colored beads fall through his fingers. It was enough to break the spell and the crowd moved forward as a group, gathering with excitement around the trinkets.

The sailors jumped from the boats onto the bank and fanning out they quickly encircled the group, blocking any means of escape.

64

As their tapaithooks drew closer to the entrance to the river, Daygon could see the tall mast, with a dirty white flag fluttering in the breeze at the top, above the trees at the bend in the river. Beads of sweat trickled over his brow into his eyes, blurring his vision, but it seemed the ship had stopped moving. He knew it was close to where the coastal camp was built. He was worried. This was a new threat, and he was not there to deal with it. He was afraid for his people. He hoped nothing happened before he got there.

"Harder," he grunted to Pugathoite, as he dug even deeper into the water to push against the strengthening river current. The muscles in his shoulders and arms burned with the exertion. The fear churning deep in his chest, where his heart was pounding like a fleeing rabbit, pushed him on.

His tapaithook rounded the bend first, in time for him to see the smaller boats reach the beach. Keeping his eye on them as he paddled, he saw one of the strangers stand in the front of one of the small boats and toss something toward the band members standing along the riverbank. Then a warning cry came from high in the mast of the large boat anchored in the middle of the river. They had been spotted.

Some of the newcomers, who had climbed out of the small boats, turned to look at them and then continued up the bank and formed a circle around the band standing in the clearing. Daygon noticed they were pointing long sticks at his people. The sticks didn't have a point at the end like an aaduth, but he knew they must be some kind of weapon. His worst fears were being realized. He had to get ashore.

He pulled hard on his paddle and turned the tapaithook toward the riverbank. When it touched the rivers edge, he and his companion, Pugathoite, grabbed their hathemays and began to run toward the camp. The brothers followed close behind them.

Breathing heavily, they reached the clearing and burst through the low bushes, with arrows notched. One of the strangers turned and pointed the stick he was carrying. Fire and smoke burst from the end of it, followed by a loud bang. Daygon heard the scream of pain from Pugathoite and turned to see blood pouring from a jagged hole in his shoulder as he squirmed in agony on the ground.

A group of crows clawed their way into the air in panic and winged away toward the distant hills.

Daygon turned back to the clearing in confusion. What was this firestick that could do that to a man from such a distance? How could they possibly fight this?

He stared into the end of many firesticks and let the hathemay slip from his fingers. "Don't shoot at them," he shouted to the men in the circle who were standing with notched arrows in their hathemays.

Women and children were screaming and crying in terror as they huddled together on the ground. His eyes searched the crowd and found Shandowee. She was holding Gadedoo at her side, doing her best to shelter him from this danger. Anger washed over him and he considered rushing this enemy, but reason prevailed, and he stood there helpless, the nails of his clenched fists cutting into his flesh. He knew there was nothing they could do, they were completely at the mercy of these strangers.

Two of the newcomers left the circle and ran toward them with long knives in their hands. They motioned for Daygon and the other two to join the rest of the band inside the circle, pushing them to hurry them along. Pugathoite was left bleeding on the ground. He no longer moved, and he had ceased to moan. Daygon feared his journey had already begun.

Daygon looked at Meroobish across the crowd. "Should we resist?" he shouted.

"They will kill us all," Meroobish replied.

Daygon nodded, knowing he was right.

"We will wait and see what they want," he announced to the terrified crowd. "Don't do anything to antagonize them.

Just as he spoke, one of the young band members grabbed his new wife's hand and ran for the shelter of the woods.

"No," shouted Daygon, remembering the ceremony he had performed for them just days ago. "No," he shouted again.

Another loud bang rang through the air and rattled off the hillside as a firestick spat fire and smoke, and the man tumbled forward onto his face. His wife hesitated for a moment, looked around wildly, and then bolted into the woods as another firestick spoke, ripping through the trees where she was last seen.

The Beothuk fell silent in disbelief. The only sound was the Buggishamen (white man) talking to each other. Then they began to separate the women and children from the men, who they pushed roughly to the ground. Two of the Buggishamen began binding the hands of the Beothuk men in front of them while one of their companions held the tip of a blade to their throat to control them. Another gathered their hathemays and aaduths, broke them into pieces and threw them on the cooking fire that was smoldering in the clearing.

Others were searching the mamateeks and tossing whatever they found through the doors. All the food and the furs from the drying racks and the storeroom were piled on the ground in the clearing. At the riverbank, two of the Buggishamen were punching holes in the tapaithooks so they couldn't be used.

From his knees, Daygon looked around in disbelief. A few hours ago, he had been thinking how peaceful the summer camp was. Now these strangers were destroying it all. They were more powerful than the Shannok. There was no way to fight these Buggishaman with their firesticks.

Perhaps they only wanted the food and furs, he thought. Maybe they just bound us to keep us from fighting, he reasoned.

While he watched, the row boats were loaded with the food and furs and rowed out to the bigger boat. Everything was lifted into the big boat and the two row boats returned.

A few moments later a long rope was brought from one of the row boats and he and nine other men were attached to it. Another rope was used to attach the remaining eight men and boys together.

Then they were prodded to their feet, handed some of the remaining furs and food each, and pulled toward the boats. Those who resisted felt the point of the Buggishamen's knives. One of the larger Buggishamen swung a long whip over his

217

head and let the tip snap on their bare backs to keep them moving. He was the one who had walked the line looking at each of the band members and had old Tammerdowitt pulled out and dragged over to the women. The stick the old man always used to help him stand still lay on the ground. It was now in two pieces.

The women began to wail, and the children cried.

Daygon glanced back at Shandowee and saw the tears on her cheeks as she hugged Gadedoo to her side. "Be strong," he yelled, trying hard to sound braver than he felt. He stumbled as he turned back and winced as he felt the sting of the lash across his shoulders. The humiliation and helplessness he felt had a sharper edge than the whip's sting. He was their leader and he could do nothing for them. He bowed his head and followed the man attached to the rope ahead of him.

They reached the edge of the riverbank and were herded into the waiting rowboats and forced to sit on the floor. A heavily bearded Buggishamen began to row toward the ship. Daygon sat with band members on each side, staring into the mouth of a firestick no more than the width of his hand from his face. He forced himself not to look back at the camp.

"Where do you think they are taking us?" asked Modthamook, who was sitting on his left side.

"I don't know," Daygon replied. "At least they left our women and children. They should be safe."

"But they've taken all their food and destroyed the tapaithooks."

"They can make more."

"We must watch for our chance to escape," muttered Meroobish on his right. "We will kill all of these Buggishamen as soon as we get a chance."

65

At the head of the bay a large river flowed from the thick forest. Captain Gaspar ordered the sails trimmed and sailors ran up the rigging toward Paublo standing in the barrel. He watched as they deftly ran out the crossbeams and dropped some of the sails to slow the ship as it turned into the river. Looking upriver, Paublo spotted several trails of smoke spiraling up through the trees, a sure sign there were natives ahead.

As the ship began rounding the first bend Paublo spotted the tepees of the native village, the source of the smoke. A large group of them was standing at the edge of the riverbank watching them approach.

He called down to the captain, who was standing on the bridge, to let him know.

A few minutes later, the ship dropped anchor in the middle of the river and the rowboats were lowered into the water. Paublo knew how this was going to end. He felt a dread in his stomach as he watched events unfolding from his vantage point. Glancing down, he saw Bo standing near the hatch door staring at the shoreline. He wondered if someday Bo would run.

The bag of trinkets, thrown up on the clearing, spilled some of the colored beads and shiny metals, easily distracting the natives and allowing the soldiers and sailors to surround the group unnoticed.

Paublo looked over his shoulder and saw two native canoes approaching from downriver. He cupped his hands around his mouth and shouted a warning to those on the shore. The four natives reached the shore, scrambled from their canoes, and ran through the underbrush toward the clearing.

The puff of smoke from one of the soldier's guns, followed by one of the running natives tumbling to the ground, halted their mad rush.

Bo had climbed the ropes and stood on the crossbeam just below him. Paublo looked at him. His dark face was a mask of anger and his knuckles were white where he gripped the ropes.

Turning back, Paublo was in time to see another of the natives shot as two of them bolted for the safety of the woods. He could see the head of the other native running through the woods, escaping the second shot. He found himself rooting for them. He suspected Bo did as well.

221

Nothing in his life had prepared him for this, or anything remotely like this. These people were being murdered like animals. He had on occasion seen animals killed, but never a person. This was not what he had expected when he had boarded this ship. The sense of excitement and adventure that had filled him the day they set sail was now gone. He just wanted to go home to Maria.

66

Standing at the tiller, Gaspar watched the natives seated on the floor of his rowboat. He had noticed how the others seemed to defer to the one with the blue and black feathers woven into the top of his long braid. He suspected he was their leader. Several times their eyes had met and held. There was a strength behind those eyes. This one would have to be watched closely, he thought. On the other hand, he would undoubtedly fetch a good price in the marketplace.

Sitting next to him was the biggest of the captives. He was head and shoulders above the rest, probably about the size of Cook. He was without doubt the strongest of them. He'd been tied with extra rope to ensure he was properly restrained and posed no danger to Gaspar's men. With that kind of strength, he would make an excellent field worker, could probably match a small horse.

The others were a mixed lot of men and boys, most of them were bare chested, wearing only leggings or cloths. None of them wore anything on their feet. All of them had red stain on their bodies and clothing just as the previous fifty-seven had. *There must be many of them on this land*, he thought. *It will be worth returning.*

Gaspar braced his feet as the rowboat bumped the side of the ship. Reaching out, he grabbed the dangling ropes, swung onto the rope ladder and climbed up and over the rail onto the deck. He strode to his cabin, leaving the supervision of loading the newly obtained cargo to his men. He noticed Bo standing near the rail watching him. Unintentionally, his hand touched the coiled whip hanging from his belt.

Cook, who had remained on the ship, followed him with a tray of hot food, placed it on his table and left him to it. The smell of the freshly cooked caribou filled the cabin and his empty stomach rumbled in anticipation.

Gaspar picked up the parchment commission signed by King Manuel and looked at it thoughtfully. The directive was to seek out new lands and lay claim for the kingdom of Portugal. It also awarded him a share of any profits realized from the voyage.

He had already made landfall twice on this new land and left the Portuguese flag as notification to others that the land was now under their claim. The slaves currently being stored in the hold would realize a nice return, and those, along with the fifty-seven already sent back to Terceira with Miguel and Antonyo would more than ensure the profitability of the trip. He would definitely return here next year. He smiled in satisfaction and pulled out the chair to his table. He wondered how Miguel's return trip was going. He hoped they didn't run into any bad weather, not with Antonyo's improvised mast.

The question that troubled him was, should he turn back now or continue south for a while longer? There was still more of this land that was uncharted, and he had plenty of supplies to feed his men and the captives. The land promised to provide plenty of game if he should run short and it would be an easy matter to replenish the food and water supply. Much of the summer still lay ahead so there certainly was no time restraint on him. He decided he would sail further south.

Sitting at the table, he dipped into the steaming hot stew Cook had made from the meat of the caribou taken from the previous natives. The meat was tender and required little effort to chew. It had a gamy taste that lingered in his mouth. The thought occurred to him that hunting those animals might be good sport.

The men who had cut the tree for Antonyo's mast had reported seeing a large herd of these animals covering a bog, just inland from the beach. Even though they had travelled considerably further south, he suspected those animals were common to all these woods. Young Paublo had also reported seeing herds of the animals as they sailed here. He decided to stay another day and lead a hunt. The meat would feed his remaining twenty-four-man crew for the rest of the voyage and would also provide some extra food for the natives below deck. They had to be taken care of until they got to market to ensure the best price.

He wiped the dried biscuit around the bowl to soak up the last of the stew and popped it into his mouth. Pushing the bowl aside, he reached behind him and pulled the logbook from the shelf. There was much to enter for this day.

67

Bragadessh and twelve other men had left the camp three days earlier to hunt for caribou. It had been a good hunt and they were now returning to camp, each carrying half a caribou slung over his shoulders. The meat would be welcomed by the band and would serve to help them get through the long snow season. He also had to store food for his three children and Taddowish to live here at the coast.

He had tried, unsuccessfully, to convince Daygon to join the hunt. He wished his brother had been there. It had been some time since they had hunted together, and he missed the companionship. They would have to do this soon, since he was not returning to the snow camp with Daygon and the rest of the band.

The morning was overcast but the late spring winds had a subtle warmth that hinted summer would soon arrive. Buds had begun to open and curl into leaves on the birch trees that lined the path. Summer birds had returned and fluttered through the high branches, following the line of men trudging through the woods.

Bragadessh, from his place near the centre of the column, heard a commotion at the front of the line and shifted his load further back on his shoulders to allow him to lift his head. The dried blood had caked on his shoulders and neck and he felt a fresh trickle on his bare back as he pushed the caribou back.

One of the young women from the camp, carrying her child in the hood of her cloak, was crying loudly and waving her hands wildly as she talked to the men in the front. Bragadessh, along with the others near him, dropped his meat and hurried to where she was standing.

As he reached the front of the line, he heard the woman screaming hysterically, "They took them. They took them all."

One of the men gripped her by the arms and shook her. "What are you saying, woman? You are not making any sense. Stop crying and tell us what happened."

"They took all the men except old Tammerdowitt.

"Who? The Shannok?" asked Bragadessh.

"No, not the Shannok," she sobbed. "Worse."

"Then who?" asked the man gripping her arm.

"It was Buggishamen. There were many of them. They came from the sea on a large boat."

"Took them where?"

"On the big boat. They took all our food as well. They are leaving with the men." The child who had been asleep in her hood began to scream, adding to the noise.

"Where is Daygon?" asked Bragadessh loudly, fearing the answer.

"He is with them. They tied their hands and forced them all to go."

"Did they fight? I know my brother would fight."

"They tried, but some of our men were killed with their firesticks. What are we going to do?" she wailed. "My husband is on that boat." She reached back, scooped up the wailing child and rocked it in her arms.

"What are firesticks?"

'They are long sticks that spit fire and smoke that can kill a man from a long way off. They are terrible. You can't run from them," she whimpered.

"Were any of the women or children hurt?"

"No," she sobbed

"We'll go and take them back," said one.

"Yes," shouted several, restlessly shifting their feet and brandishing the weapons in their hands.

"What about the firesticks?"

"We will take them from them," said another.

"They destroyed our tapaithooks," said the woman. "They punched holes in them so they can't be used.

"Where is the rest of the band?"

"They are hiding in the woods. They are safe."

"Where are the Buggishamen now?"

"They are all back on the boat."

"Has the boat left?"

"No. It is still there in the middle of the river."

"Leave the animals here," ordered Bragadessh. "She can stay with them until the others come. Let's go and see this boat."

The men nodded in agreement and fell in behind Bragadessh as he began to run.

Standing next to the caribou, the woman watched them go and bent her tear-stained face to nuzzle her little one. "It will be alright now, little one," she whispered.

68

Daygon was chained to a metal loop fastened to the wall of the ship, lying on a narrow wooden shelf with his feet pointing out toward the center of the room. His shoulders touched the men chained on each side of him. The ceiling was no more than the width of his hand above him. Each time he tried to lift his head he bumped it off the rough lumber. The short chain attached to the shackles they had fastened to his wrists only allowed his arms to reach his chest. His feet were tied to the edge of the shelf with rope that was too tight. Already his toes were tingling with numbness.

Below him were other shelves stacked with the other men of the band. He could not see them in the thick darkness, but he could hear them. Some were cursing the Buggishamen, some were calling the names of their family, others were crying out to the Great Spirit for help. The despair in the room was as heavy as the darkness. These men only knew the freedom of the open spaces. This confinement was causing many to panic. Things were breaking down quickly.

Across the small walkway that provided space for the Buggishamen to walk the length of the room, were the feet of other men. Daygon had seen them being chained before the door was closed and all light taken from the room.

Some of the older boys were sobbing, none of them understood what was happening. There had been no sign of the Buggishamen since they had chained them up. That was a long time ago.

Daygon wondered whether it was day or night now. He had lost track of time and there was no way to tell. He thought they might be in the second day.

Already the tiny room stank. The terror of the close confinement in the dark had served to make many of them sick. There was nowhere to vomit, and the contents of their stomachs dripped on the men on the shelves below. This was mixed with urine and feces from those who could no longer hold it. The air was heavy and made breathing difficult. He fought to supress the urge to empty the contents of his stomach. He did not want it to fall on the men below.

The darkness was filled with moaning and curses of the men who saw no escape from this hopeless situation. Boys cried out the names of their mothers, men the names of their wives and children. Others just cried, lost in their fear and misery.

Daygon tried to push his mind away from the pain of his bindings and the prickling in his back where splinters from the rough wood entered his skin each time he tried to shift his weight to keep his legs from cramping. He thought of Shandowee and little Gadedoo. He wondered if he would get to meet the new little one. His mind turned to his brother. He wondered if his hunting group had returned from the caribou hunt yet. He knew they would try and help them if they had. He hoped the boat didn't leave before that happened. It was the only chance they had.

He had no idea why they were taken or what would happen to them, regardless of how many times the question came out of the darkness around him. It made him feel inadequate and a failure. This was twice this season he had failed to protect the band. He felt unworthy of the title, chief.

He lifted his head and banged it against the low ceiling in frustration. He felt a warm trickle of blood slip down his forehead. The throbbing pain it caused was barely noticeable amidst the other pain and discomfort he was feeling. He squirmed to try and find some small relief.

Somehow we will find a way to break free and kill these Buggishamen, he thought, as a tear escaped and found its way down his cheek.

Then out of the darkness from below him came the deep melodious voice of Meroobish as he began to sing a battle song. Gradually more of the captives joined in. Daygon appreciated his strength, a strength he did not feel himself. *Maybe he should be chief*, he thought.

233

69

Bragadessh kept running, ignoring the pain in his chest and legs, leading the men toward the beach. He wondered who these Buggishamen were and why they had taken all the men from the camp. What were they planning to do with them? With his brother out there, he knew he had to do something to try and get them back. He knew Daygon and the others were counting on him. He determined not to let them down.

He never altered his speed when a startled animal crashed through the bushes at the side of the path. He just pushed on toward the camp.

Soon the woods began to thin out and the path widened, signalling they were nearing the camp. Bragadessh slowed when he reached the place where raw stumps stuck out of the ground, left by the band when they cut down trees to repair the mamateeks and drying racks. As he continued walking, he caught glimpses of the big boat out in the middle of the river. It had several tall posts sticking into the air with cloth hanging from them. The tops of them were higher than the trees. He wondered what they were for.

He was relieved it was still there. As long as it was, there was still a chance they could do something to save his brother and the other band members.

The men grouped around him at the edge of the trees that ringed the clearing, some kneeling, some crouching. There was enough cover to keep them hidden from view from the boat.

In the clearing, smoke still drifted lazily into the sky from the cook fire, although the cooking pot lay upended on the ground. Near each mamateek items of clothing and food baskets lay strewn in front of the doors. The bodies of Pugathoite and the other young man lay where they had been killed. Seagulls and crows had found them. They did not drive them away for fear of alerting the Buggishamen.

They stared silently at the large boat, anchored in the middle of the river, that held their friends and family members somewhere inside. They had never seen a boat so big. It could carry many men, just like the woman had said.

"How do we get out there?" someone finally asked. "The tapaithooks will not carry us with those holes in them."

"There is no time to repair them," said another, "The boat could leave anytime."

"How many of you can swim?" asked Bragadessh.

Only three hands went up.

"So that makes only four of us."

"Hardly enough to take all of the Buggishaman."

"There's always some of them walking around. They will see us coming."

"Look, there is someone in the basket at the top of that tall pole."

"He will see us for sure."

"Not if we go in the dark."

"We may not have that long. They could leave."

"I don't think they will leave in the dark. They cannot see how to get down river."

"I agree. They have left the small boats in the water. They are not going anywhere yet."

"There are two tapaithooks upriver. Go get them," Bragadessh ordered two of the men. "You should be back before it gets light again. We will stay and keep watch."

The men hurried away upriver as the last light of the day was drawn over the horizon. The others made busy preparing places to sleep.

70

First light began to color the dark sky with a pale-yellow brush. Bragadessh had not slept. He had watched the dim lights of the big boat, anchored in the river, all night long. A short time ago he had seen one of the Buggishamen walk around the deck of the boat putting out the lights. Another younger one had climbed the ropes to the top of the tallest pole where he climbed into a small basket. The two smaller boats were still tied to the side of the bigger one. The men he had sent upriver for the tapaithooks had not yet returned. He expected them to be back soon.

After darkness had fallen last night, they had recovered the bodies of the two band members lying in the clearing. They dragged them into the woods and covered them in boughs to protect them until they freed the rest of the band being held prisoner on the big boat.

Toorett stirred next to him, stretched and sat up. "You did not sleep, my friend?" he asked.

"No, sleep would not come."

"We will get your brother back today," Toorett said.

Bragadessh was about to reply when he was interrupted by the returning men carrying the tapaithooks on their shoulders. He waved them into a crouch as they crossed the last ground to their hiding place behind the evergreen trees.

"It will not be so easy to get to the boat now that the night has passed," he said. "The tapaithooks will not carry all of us. Some will have to be in the water holding to the sides."

"Maybe we should go down river and come up from behind."

"There is a boy up there," said Bragadessh, pointing to the top of the boat's tall pole. "From there he can see for a great distance all around. We would be discovered before we reached the boat."

"Look," said Toorett, pointing.

All eyes turned toward the big boat. A group of the Buggishamen gathered at the rail and began to climb down the ropes into one of the smaller boats in the water below.

"One, two, three, ..." Bragadessh counted aloud. "Thirteen. There are thirteen of them."

Most of them were carrying the long firesticks the woman had described.

"Are they coming for us?" asked one of the men anxiously.

"They could not have seen us," said Bragadessh.

"Perhaps they are coming for the women."

"What should we do?"

"Kill them."

"If we can do that there won't be so many left on the big boat'" said Bragadessh.

"But how? There are as many of them as us."

"And they carry their firesticks."

"We have to surprise them. They don't know we are here. That gives us the advantage."

71

Standing at the front of the gently rocking rowboat, Gaspar drew deep breaths of the quiet morning air as he surveyed the deserted beach. All the natives had run. There were only women and children and the crippled old man left so he was not worried for the safety of his men. These people were like timid animals. They ran at the slightest sign of danger. He looked up at the partially clear sky. It promised to be a dry day. He smiled in anticipation of the hunt.

The bow of the boat ground on the sand and he jumped. The only sound was the splashing of his men's feet as they followed him over the side into the shallow water.

The men pulled the boat on to the shore and unloaded their supplies.

"You four stay here," commanded Gaspar, indicating the sailors who had rowed the boat. "We should be back before dark. There will be fresh caribou meat for tonight," he added with a grin.

Once the men were ready, Gasper set out across the clearing, past the deserted mamateeks and toward the treeline, with Fernam walking at his side until they reached the edge of the woods. Here the path narrowed and only allowed room for them to pass in single file, so Fernam dropped back behind his captain.

Bragadessh and the other Beothuk watched them pass from their hiding places amongst the trees.

"They split up," whispered Toorett. "There are only nine."

Bragadessh nodded and smiled. "If they stay on this path they will find our caribou. That will distract them. We will get them there." He tightened his grip on the handle of the Dthoonanven hanging from his belt. He would put it to good use before this day was done, he thought.

He saw the battle fervor in the eyes of the men gathered around him. Today these Buggishamen would pay for what they had done.

To Toorett he said, "Get to the caribou before them and warn the woman. Make it look like an animal has eaten one of the caribou. That will make them think they have been there for a while. Wait for us there. We will follow them at a distance."

Toorett ran into the woods.

72

The four sailors on the beach secured the rowboat, unloaded their lunch supplies and walked up the beach to the edge of the woods. It would be a quiet day. A day with no work. There weren't many of those, so they were meant to be savored.

They carried their supplies just above the high-water mark outlined by the empty broken shells washed up by the sea.

"Let's gather some dry wood and get a fire started," said Alvaro, as he began to scoop a shallow hole in the dark sand. Lopo, Bernaldo and Luis pushed through the low brush and soon returned with an armload of dry sticks each, dumping them in a pile near the hole Alvaro had dug.

Soon Alvaro had a fire going over which he hung two of the fish they brought from the ship. Once they were roasted, they ate their fill and then sat around the crackling fire watching the ship swing lazily on it's anchor, pushed by the river current and the light wind.

"What do you think of those natives?" asked Lopo, leaning back on his elbow as he picked the stray bits of fish from his teeth with a sharpened splinter from the firewood.

"What do you mean?"

"What I mean is, do you think they are fighters?" replied Lopo, spitting a bone into the nearby underbrush.

"Not a chance," laughed Bernaldo heartedly. "Did you see their primitive bows and stone axes? What do you think they could do with those?"

"They were too scared to fight back. Did you see their faces when the gun was fired?" asked Alvaro.

"First time they saw one, I expect," muttered Luis with a wide yawn.

"Think we should take turns guarding?" asked Lopo, glancing over his shoulder into the low brush at the edge of the woods.

"What for? We have all the men of the tribe on the ship. There's only women and children and one crippled old man left, and I'm guessing they've run deep into the woods by now. There's nothing to worry about here."

"S'pose you're right, Bernaldo," said Lopo, and he stretched out on the sand near the others. He squirmed his shoulders and pushed his heels into the sand to make himself more comfortable, folded his hands behind his head and stared up at the wispy clouds drifting across the sky above him. It had been a long time since he'd been able to relax like this. Soon the heavy breathing signaled his companions were asleep and he let his droopy eyelids close and he joined them.

73

Fernam looked up from the ground just in time to avoid walking into the captain who had suddenly stopped in the middle of the path. Stepping to the side, he saw what had caught the captain's attention. Just a few steps ahead of them a bunch of caribou carcass were piled in the path. Each one had been cut into two pieces. It looked to him like there were at least a half dozen and they looked fresh. It would take a large group of natives to carry that many. He looked around warily, scanning the thick woods for any movement, as he handed the captain his gun that he had been carrying.

"I wonder if the women did this as some kind of offering to get their men back," Gasper mumbled softly, eying the surrounding woods suspiciously for any movement.

Fernam nodded in agreement. "Maybe they were watching us from the shelter of the forest. Guess they could be out there somewhere," he said, swivelling all the way around as he scanned the woods."

Seeing no movement, they slowly approached the mound of meat. One of the carcasses had been pulled to the side and appeared to have been partially eaten.

"Must have been here for a while," observed Fernam. "Guess the natives are long gone if a wild animal felt comfortable doing that. Relax, men," he said, "There's no one out there."

The men lowered their guns and stepped forward gathering around the caribou, some standing, some down on one knee, examining the carcasses.

Bragadessh smiled with satisfaction as he watched the Buggishamen lower their firesticks and crowd around the caribou. The dead caribou had drawn them in perfectly. He couldn't have planned it any better, he thought. He glanced around the small clearing where his men had hidden themselves and nodded. Each of them now stood with hathemays drawn. He had instructed them to pick their targets so each would have a different Buggishaman. He stepped onto the path behind them, pulled the string on his hathemay tight and whistled. Everyone released their arrows. Each embedded in its target. His hit the big man in the centre of the group, the one who seemed to be their leader.

Gasper grunted as the arrow pierced his back. Fernam stumbled to his knees next to him, blood spurting around the shaft of the arrow that protruded from both sides of his neck. Men were falling all around him as the air was split with primeval screams from the rushing natives, all of them brandishing knives, axes and spears.

One of the soldiers managed to get off a shot from his musket before they were overwhelmed by the charging mob. The shot tore away the chest of the closest native and he collapsed on the ground, his feet kicking wildly in his final death throes.

Gaspar tried to raise his gun, but his left arm would not obey. He let it slip from his fingers to the ground and reached for the dagger at his belt with his right hand. Around him, the men who had survived the first wave of arrows were engaged in hand to hand combat with the crazed natives. He could see it was one-sided since all his men were already wounded. To his right, one of the natives sat astride the chest of a seaman with his two hands firmly around his throat. Gaspar plunged his dagger into his side and twisted. The native fell over into a spreading pool of his own blood.

Gaspar reached down his hand to help the seaman up just as the wounded man croaked a muffled warning from his tortured throat. Gaspar half turned and raised his arm to defend himself against the descending axe, taking the full blow on his forearm. The blade bit deep into the bone. He looked at it curiously. Unable to free the axe, the native released its handle and pulled a knife from the sheath at his side. With an upward thrust he plunged it deep into Gaspar's chest. He was close enough for Gaspar to smell his hot breath and look into his dark eyes.

Gaspar's knees buckled as his strength flowed from him and he collapsed to his knees on the ground next to the still body of his helmsman. Waves of pain racked his body and then darkness swirled over him as his arms could no longer support him and he fell forward.

74

Lopo opened his eyes to the flutter of birds in the bushes behind him. Above him the sky had turned more grey than blue. He lifted his head and glanced around at his companions. They had all slept through the afternoon. Out in the river, the ship rocked gently on its anchor. He noticed with relief their boat still lay on its side on the beach where they had left it. *At least the captain hadn't returned and found them all asleep,* he thought. That would not have been good. He was not anxious to test the captain's anger. He had not seen it often, once in fact, but once had been enough.

"Hey, wake up," he said.

The others stirred and sat up.

"It'll be getting dark soon," Lopo said. "The hunting party should be here anytime now."

"Best get the fire going again," said Bernaldo, giving an exaggerated yawn."

"Luis, go back in there and find some dry sticks," said Alvaro, nodding his head in the direction of the woods.

Luis pushed to his feet, stretched and shuffled into the nearby trees, mumbling softly when he thought he was out of earshot. "Luis, you get the wood. Luis do this. Luis do that. Its always got to be Luis. Why can't anyone else do anything around here?"

He had gathered an armful of dry sticks and was stooping to pick up one more when he heard the snap of a twig directly behind him. He froze as he felt a presence at his back. The stick slipped from his fingers as he grabbed for the knife at his side. Before he could turn, a hand covered his, preventing him from drawing the knife. Dirty red-brown fingers covered his face and pulled his head back as a knee was pushed against his back. He stared into his killer's dark eyes as a blade that he expected might be his own was drawn across his exposed throat.

"Let's get the other three," whispered Bragadessh as he let the limp Buggishaman slump to the ground.

They crept silently through the woods at the edge of beach until they had positioned themselves directly next to the three sailors sitting near the smouldering embers of a fire. Flies buzzed around a half-eaten piece of fish that must be the remains of their lunch, Bragadessh noticed. There was only one firestick and that was propped against a tree trunk, too far away for any of the Buggishamen to reach. *This will be easy*, he thought.

"Do it quickly," whispered Bragadessh. "We don't want to raise the alarm on the big boat.

"Why is Luis taking so long?" asked Alvaro, as he threw the last couple of sticks on the fire, raising a shower of flankers that drifted skyward.

"Did you ever know him to rush at anything?" laughed Lopo. "You see how he shuffles. That's his fastest speed."

"Never," agreed Alvaro, as he rummaged in his bag for something else to eat. "That's as fast as he can think. He's probably already forgotten what he went back there for. Dumb as....."

The Beothuk sprang from their hiding place in the bushes and rushed them, overwhelming them before they had a chance to realize what was happening. It ended quickly and the bodies were dragged into the undergrowth at the edge of the woods.

"Build their fire up so those on the big boat won't get suspicious," ordered Bragadessh. In his mind he counted off the thirteen. "Stay low and don't let anyone out there see you. Put on that one's hat and tunic in case they are watching."

75

Bo watched from the corner of the raised hatch as Diego walked across the deck, lit a cigarette, leaned against the rail and stared at the water below. Earlier in the day he'd made up his mind that this was the night he was going to escape. Most of the crew was with the captain on the hunting trip and there would be no better time. The second rowboat was still in the water waiting for him to use. It would be easy.

He knew this wasn't his homeland but maybe it was close. First, he had to escape from these people. The rest he would worry about later.

He wished he could say goodbye to Paublo but that would only jeopardize his escape.

Seeing Diego there alone at the rail was too good a chance to miss. It was as if the Gods were offering it to him. He had to kill him before he left.

Quietly, he placed the bag with the shirt and boots he had taken from below on the deck, and quickly went back down the stairs to the galley. He selected a long knife from the rack over the worktable. Cook had gone below to the storage room and hadn't yet returned. He grabbed a several dried biscuits and hurried up the stairs.

Stepping through the open hatch door, he glanced around the corner of the wall. Diego was still there, looking over the rail. He was sure everyone else was below deck. He ran across the deck, his bare feet making no sound.

He was but a step away when Diego flicked the cigarette into the water and turned away from the rail.

"What are you doing here?" he said with surprise as Bo closed the distance, clamped his hand over his mouth and pushed the knife into his throat. All resistance drained from Diego as the blood spurted from his body. Bo lifted him and pushed him over the rail, hoping there was no one near to hear the splash. There was nothing he could do about the blood. He hoped he was well away before it was found.

He ran to the other side, grabbed his bag as he passed the hatch, and scrambled down the ropes to the rowboat. Using the bloodied knife, he cut the rope, took his seat and began to row. Staying close to the side of the ship, he maneuvered around the stern and headed for the opposite shore of the river from where the Indian camp was. He did not want to chance running into the returning hunters or any natives that might still be there.

He had no idea where he was going or what he would do next, but he had escaped and that was all that mattered. He felt a weight lift and a smile crease his face as he rowed. He was free.

Lights flickered in the near darkness as Francisco lit the ships lanterns on the other side of the boat.

The rowboat bumped the shore and he scrambled out, pushing the boat back into the current. He stood watching for a minute as the river carried it into the darkness toward the open water of the bay. For a moment he wondered if he might need it later, then told himself he would stick to land from now on, wherever it took him.

Sitting on the bank, he pulled on the shirt and boots, stood to his feet and took one last look at the ship. He listened for a moment as the faint chant of the natives echoed across the dark water.

"Kelanti," he said aloud, turned and walked into the forest.

76

Paublo stood near the big chart table and looked around the captain's quarters. Everything seemed to be in its proper place. He had not had to clean the quarters for some time since he had been on lookout most of the time since the barrel was installed. It was what he'd been brought on the ship for in the beginning, but he liked the lookout position better. He was grateful the captain had agreed to bring him on this voyage. Where else would he have had such great experiences as the past weeks had brought, he thought as he replaced the captain's logbook on the shelf. He stared at the large chart spread on the tabletop and wondered how to read it. There were markings and notes all over it. He guessed the captain was mapping their route. As grateful as he was, he was troubled with the way things had turned out with the slaves. It had soured the trip for him and taken away the joy of sailing that he had so longed for on the farm back on Terceira.

As he stepped out on the deck, he could hear the moaning of the captured slaves in the hold below. He would get a share of the money they would bring at the auction. He knew that would help his parents in running the farm, but he no longer wanted it. It would feel like dirty money to him.

The hatch had been left open to air out the stink below decks. He wrinkled his nose at the stench as he passed. Then, from the darkness below came a low haunting chant that raised the fine hairs on the back of his neck. He wondered what the words meant. The noise rose in volume until it seemed they were all singing.

Standing there, he felt a stirring deep inside as he listened. It served to fuel the doubt that he felt. He knew the general attitude of the crew was that these captives were not in the same category as them, that they were beneath them and meant to be exploited, that they were little more than animals. He knew this was not true. They were people just like him and should be treated that way, but there was no way he could defy his captain.

Other than the sounds from the hatch, the evening was quiet, almost too quiet. The ship barely moved on its anchor. Looking toward the beach, he could just make out where the sailors waited for the hunting party to return. He could barely see the flickering fire, but no movement near it. He thought it odd that the four of them would sleep all day and not be moving around the beach at this late hour.

He decided to climb to the barrel to have a better look. As he swung out onto the ropes, he nodded to the two sailors who were leaning on the far rail, quietly talking. Everyone else seemed to be below deck.

He had become much more sure-footed in the days since leaving Terceira. The ropes were as familiar to him now as walking the deck and he ascended them with confidence and speed. Reaching the barrel, he swung over the edge and stood on the narrow floor. Far below he could see the heads of the two sailors standing at the rail. Francisco was walking around the deck holding the torch he was using to light the lanterns spaced along the rail.

Turning toward the shore, he searched around the flickering fire on the beach. There was no sign of the sailors. He squinted his eyes against the darkness that was beginning to cloak the beach. The rowboat was no longer there, and his first thought was that the hunting party had returned, but he wondered why they would have left the fire in. He scanned the water between the ship and the beach, but the boat was nowhere to be seen. Uneasiness began to creep into his mind. Something was wrong. Something didn't feel right.

77

The Beothuk sat on the ground further down the beach from the fire in the undergrowth that grew up to the edge of the sand. They quietly stared out at the big boat. Each of them thinking of the battle and the two band members they had lost to the Buggishaman. They knew it was likely they would lose more before their friends were rescued, but it was something that must be done.

"What do we do now?" asked Toorett.

"We use their boat to get out there," announced Bragadessh.

Some of the men nodded, others looked at him with doubt clearly registering in their eyes.

"That won't work. They will see us coming and use their firesticks to kill us," one of them voiced the thought of the others.

"We'll wait a little longer until darkness comes. They won't leave without the others."

"Did you see how they rowed that boat. It was not like our tapaithooks."

"I did. One man to each paddle."

"We'll manage. Its just a short distance."

"Look, one of them is leaving," said Toorett.

They watched as a dark-skinned man quickly descended the ropes and clambered into the small boat. He awkwardly rowed the boat that was meant for two rowers around the big boat, and disappeared on the other side.

"Where's he going?"

"Looks like the other shore."

The battle song came wafting across the water, shattering the still evening air. The group fell silent at the confirmation their friends were still alive. One of them hummed along softly.

"Look," said Toorett. "The other boat is floating downriver."

"It looks empty," said another. "No one is steering it."

"He must have got out on the other side and let it go."

"Forget him. He's only one. Let's go," said Bragadessh, looking up at the evening sky. "The Great Spirit is giving us clouds for cover. We must make no noise until we are on the boat."

Standing in the shallow water, Toorett held the Buggishaman's boat steady until the other ten band members had climbed aboard. Two of them grasped a paddle each and quietly slipped them in the water. Short ropes already attached the paddles to short sticks protruding from the sides of the boat. Toorett pushed the boat away from the shore and climbed in.

They began to pull on the paddles and the boat began to turn in a circle.

"Pull together," whispered Toorett, "You're just fighting each other."

The two men stopped rowing.

"Now," said Toorett. "Again, again."

This time they moved in a straighter line. At the back, Bragadessh gripped the long handle attached to the large board that was fastened to the back of the boat. He found if he pushed it to one side or the other, he could change the direction of the boat, once it began to move forward.

He aimed for the back of the big boat. It looked like they would be able to row underneath the tall deck that overhung the water. They could hide there until they were sure no one had seen them and then find a way to climb aboard.

They reached the big boat without incident. The paddles were lifted from the water and carefully and quietly placed across the seats. Using their hands to keep from bumping the sloped side, they maneuvered the small boat underneath the overhang.

Standing at the back of the boat, Bragadessh listened to the battle song. It struck pride and confidence in the heart of each of the warriors. It was just what they needed to get their courage up to face the firesticks of these Buggishamen. The men sat there quietly listening.

"They are inside the boat somewhere," whispered Toorett.

"We will find them," said Bragadessh.

The darkness of the water was pushed back by reflections of light as someone lit lanterns above them.

"We have to move around to where the ropes are hanging down the side," whispered Bragadessh. "It's the only way to get up there."

"Some of you get your hathemays ready in case there is someone looking."

"Quietly. Don't bump the boat."

78

Peering down at the deck, Paublo watched as Francisco limped to the last lantern and lit it. Then he stepped through the hatch door carrying the smouldering torch in his hand. He wondered where the rowboat from the shore was. He looked down at the side of the ship and realized the other rowboat that had been tied up there was also missing. He decided he should raise the alarm. There was something wrong, of that he was certain.

Turning back to call down to the two men who stood at the rail, he caught movement out of the corner of his eye. Looking toward the movement he gasped in surprise as several natives swarmed over the opposite rail and ran at the unsuspecting sailors, their bare feet making no sound on the wooden deck.

Shouting a warning, he watched in horror as the natives rushed the unarmed men and impaled them on their long spears before they had a chance to run.

Suddenly the air was split with the primal war cry of the victorious natives. One of them looked up at him shook his fist and screamed something. He didn't understand the words, but he knew the meaning. He ducked his head and cowered in the tiny barrel. He had no weapon, and even if he did, he knew he was no match for them. He hoped they didn't like to climb.

The war cry was taken up by the Beothuk below deck, and the natives ran for the hatch to free their friends. Paublo felt the skin on his back prickle as the war cry increased in volume. He chanced a peek over the edge of the barrel. He knew there were only eleven of them left on the ship. Counting him and the two dead sailors at the rail, that only left eight. This was not going to be a fair fight.

A commotion at the hatch pulled his eyes back to the deck. Francisco was being dragged up the steps by two of the natives. Another native was holding his smoldering torch. As he stepped through the hatch door the wind flared the torch into life, lighting the frightening scene.

On the deck just outside the hatch a native held each of Francisco's arms straight out from his sides, while a third placed the tip of his spear against his chest and pushed. Paublo covered his ears to block out Francisco's screams. Unable to pull his eyes away, he watched him die. He felt sorry for him. He was the first sailor he had talked to when he boarded the ship.

He crouched a little lower in the barrel. He was terrified. Now there are only seven, he thought. The only thing that would save him would be the return of the captain. He looked anxiously toward the flickering fire on the now dark beach. There was no sign of the hunting party. He shivered in fear. He did not want to die at their hands. He thought about jumping into the dark water, but he knew he would never clear the side of the ship, and it was a long way down. He wondered what had happened to Bo.

The natives crowded behind their companion with the torch and followed him back down into the hold. He wondered if he should climb down, but he knew there was nothing he could do to help the others. He decided he would stay hiding and hope they forgot he was there. He wished the captain would come back with the soldiers.

79

"What's happening?" hissed Duarte into the darkness.

"We've been boarded by more of those natives. Didn't you hear that bloodthirsty scream?"

"Where did they come from? I thought we had them all."

"They must have been hiding in the woods."

"Where is the captain and the soldiers?"

"Perhaps they got them first."

"What are we going to do?"

"How many of you are here?"

"There are three of us, four counting you. Cook is in the galley and Paublo is on deck somewhere, probably in his basket. They just dragged Francisco up the stairs. Rui and Martim were on deck earlier. They probably got them first. I don't know where the black is."

"Where is Diego?"

"Haven't seen him for a while."

"Heard him say he was going up for a smoke."

"Any of you have weapons?"

"No."

"Alright", said Duarte. "Let's get down to the cargo deck. Muskets and cutlasses are stored there in the small room off the slave room. Kegs of powder are there as well, so no torches. Be quiet if you want to live. Feel your way along the hallway and hold the shirt of the man in front."

80

"Bragadessh, is that you?" yelled Daygon from the darkness below. "We are down here at the bottom of the boat."

"Keep calling brother. I am coming," Bragadessh called in reply, with a leap in his heart as he hurried down the narrow wooden stairs following the torchbearer. Behind him he could feel the closeness of the other men as they crowded down the stairs, the battle lust now on them. His heart was leaping in his chest. He had heard his brother's voice. He was going to set him free.

As they reached the bottom of the stairs, a large shadow suddenly emerged from the darkness of the narrow hallway, a cleaver flashed in the muted light and the torchbearer screamed as his severed hand, still clutching the torch, fell to the floor at his feet.

The cleaver flashed again and Bragadessh ducked feeling his hair move as it passed over his head, followed by the gurgle as its edge found the Beothuk behind him. Bragadessh thrust his knife into the bulky chest of its bearer. Another warrior rammed his aaduth into the big man's chest, snapping off the handle as he fell. Together they finished the mountain of a Buggishaman. Bragadessh lifted his hands to his nose and sniffed. The smell of cooked food was all over them, but there was a much viler smell coming from somewhere below them.

Grabbing his knife, Bragadessh pulled it from the big Buggishaman and cut away his shirt. He handed the cloth to the moaning warrior sitting on the floor. "Wrap this around your arm to stop the bleeding," he said. "We will come back for you."

Another of his men picked up the flickering torch from the lifeless hand and they stepped over the dead Buggishaman and continued down the next stairs toward the sound of Daygon's voice and the overpowering smell.

Directly ahead, at the bottom of the stairs, was a heavy wooden door. Daygon's voice seemed to be coming from the other side of it. With the help of one of his men, Bragadessh lifted aside the thick plank placed across the door and threw it to the floor. The torchbearer pulled open the door to the narrow room and the stench momentarily halted them. Behind him, Bragadessh heard a gasp of disgust at what the Buggishaman had done to their band members.

"We have to kill them all," muttered Toorett. "They must pay for this."

"Where are you brother?" asked Bragadessh.

"Here. We are all chained to the walls."

Bragadessh stepped through the door onto the slippery deck boards, almost losing his balance on the smelly slick that immediately coated his bare feet. He grabbed a chain that was attached to the wall to catch himself. The man attached to it groaned with pain.

Immediately the room filled with shouts of relief and rattling chains at the sight of their rescuers. The noise in the confined space was deafening.

"Down here brother," shouted Daygon.

"Two of you stay here and guard the door," said Bragadessh over his shoulder as he continued along the narrow aisle until he reached his brother. "It is good to see you, brother," said Daygon as Bragadessh reached out and gripped his chained hand with both of his.

"And you my brother. Now let's get you out of here."

"Where are the Buggishamen?"

"Most of them are dead. We will find the rest, once you are free."

"I knew you would come, Bragadessh. I told them you would."

"You with the axe. See if you can break these." ordered Bragadessh. "The rest of you cut the ropes on their feet."

Moans of pain and relief accompanied the cutting of the ropes as the blood flow began to return to their swollen feet, filling them with a thousand tiny pinpricks of pain. Their chained hands wouldn't allow them to reach their feet to rub away the throbbing pain. They simply had to endure it until it passed.

The warrior went to work on the chain attaching Daygon to the wall. After five swings, each heavier than the last, it was obvious it wasn't going to work. The edge of the axe was filled with dents and the chains were barely scored.

"You need tools", said Daygon. "The Buggishamen drove those pins into the chains to fasten them. They took the tools through that door."

Toorett took the torch carrier by the arm. Pushing his way back through the crowded aisle, he led him to the small door partially hidden by the heavy wooden door that had been swung open against the wall. Half closing the heavy door, he bent and pushed the smaller one inward, then crawled through after the torch carrier. Lifting the torch above their heads, the flickering light revealed a small room filled with storage barrels and chests. Toorett stood to his feet and looked around. He looked down to see the fine black sand that had crept between his toes. It had spilled from one of the open barrels. He reached out his hand and rolled the barrel curiously, catching some of the sand in his hand as it spilled through the little hole in the side. He let it sift through his fingers, wondering why they carry sand in a barrel.

A slight movement caught his eye and he saw the Buggishamen hiding in the far corner with their backs against the wall. One of them was pointing a firestick.

"Look out," cried Toorett, as he jostled the torchbearer, causing him to lose his grip on the torch.

The torch bounced on a crate and came to rest on the black sand. Toorett heard a Buggishaman scream, then a blinding flash and searing inferno instantly destroyed everything in the room. The exploding barrels blew out the wall separating them from the chained slaves, the floor of the decks above and the side of the boat.

Debris that erupted from the hatch and splintered deck was hurled into the air, some of it whistling past Paublo and rattling off his hiding place atop the mast. He clung to the edge of the barrel and peered over it as the shock wave pounded him from below. Flames were roaring up through the hatches and new holes in the deck. No one could have survived that, he knew.

His ears rang and the heavy black smoke from the fire that was quickly engulfing the ship was burning his eyes. He couldn't think what to do. There was no way down. Even the ropes and furled sails were ablaze. He couldn't jump. He was still over the deck and would never leap out far enough to hit the water. The searing heat was warming the boards beneath his feet. Panic began to rise in his throat, and he spat the foul taste from his mouth.

Looking around wildly for some way out, he felt the ship began to list to the side. Peering over the edge he noticed the main deck was partially submerged. The ship was sinking. The water rushing into the gaping hole was pulling it over on its side. The mast was slowly tipping toward the water.

"Yes," he exclaimed with mounting hope. For a moment he slipped his hand inside his pocket and cupped the stone for luck. He wondered if he would ever see her again.

He climbed over the edge of the barrel onto the smoldering crossbeam of the mast and leaped.

81

As the leaves turned many shades of red, fall faded, taking the fishing season with it. These days she spent more time sitting on the hillside staring out at the sea, trying not to imagine what might have happened. The other two ships had returned long ago. He should have been back by now, they all said.

The icy wind pulled at her wrap, threatening to yank it from her shoulders. She gripped it more firmly, took another longing look at the distant horizon and began the long walk back to her little cottage. The cold wind penetrated her chest and wrapped its icy fingers around her saddened heart. It would not be today.

Author's Notes

Following a failed attempt in 1500, Gaspar Corte-Real along with his brother Miguel, set out in 1501 on a second exploratory voyage under commission from King Manuel of Portugal. The mission was to find a Northwest Passage to Asia.

Of the three carvels that sailed only two returned to Portugal. Gaspar and his crew were never heard off again.

In 1502 his brother Miguel took a single ship to retrace the previous year's voyage in an attempt to find Gaspar, but he also disappeared.

In 1918 a large stone, ten feet by five feet, was found near Dighton, Massachusetts where it had been sitting submerged in the Taunton River. Many inscriptions were found on this rock, one of which was the Portuguese Coat of Arms and the name Miguel Corte Real, along with the date 1511. It appears Miguel may have lived an additional nine years after his disappearance in 1502 and sailed much further south than his brother was believed to have done.

The disappearance of Gaspar has been the subject of many conjectures, and the true mystery will probably never be solved.

This is my story of what might have happened somewhere on the shores of Notre Dame Bay so many years ago, with his fateful encounter with the Beothuk nation, the island's first inhabitants.

INSCRIPTION TROUVÉE SUR LE ROCHER ASSONNET OU ROC DIGHTON

D'après le dessin fait sous la surveillance de la Société Historique de l'île de Rodas A.D. 1830.

Sketch of the markings found on the Dighton Rock

This statue of Gaspar Corte Real is standing near the Confederation Building in St. John's, Newfoundland. The inscription reads:

Gaspar Corte-Real, Portuguese Navigator.

He reached Terra Nova in the 15ᵗʰ century – at the beginning of the Era of the Great Discoveries.

From the Portuguese Fisheries Organization as an expression of gratitude on behalf of the Portuguese Grand Banks fishermen for the friendly hospitality always extended to them by the people of Terra Nova. May 1965.

Glossary of Terms

The following represents a list of Beothuk words used in this book. These were recorded by William Cormack during his many conversations with Shanawdithit.

Aaduth	*spear*
Buggishaman	*white man*
Dthoonanven	*stone axe*
Hathemay	*bow*
Tapaithook	*canoe*
Gossett	*land of the dead*
Shannok	*Mi'kmaq Indian*

Historical Characters

Several historical characters are represented in this book. As a work of historical fiction, fictional characters are used to develop a picture of the missing pieces and stories of what the lives of these historical characters might have been.

Other Books by the Author

The Red Indian series:

Red Indian – The Early Years: published March 2015.

This, the first book in the series, follows the lives of Shanawdithit's mother, Shanadee, and her family as they struggle to survive the formidable challenges mounted against them by the arrival of the early European settlers to the shores of Newfoundland.

Red Indian – The Final Days: published March 2016.

The second book in the series brings the stories of the fifteen Beothuk that Shanawdithit reported to William Cormack were living at the time she was captured. It attempts to provide some insight into what may have happened to them as they disappeared.

Red Indian – The Beginning: published July 2017.

Having no access to pen and paper, the Beothuk passed on the stories of their families by word of mouth. The third book in this series records the stories of the ancestors of Shanadee and Kirradittii, as told so many times around the family campfire.

Bloody Point: published July 2019.

Legend has it that Hants Harbour, a small community on the eastern shore of the island of Newfoundland, was the scene of a terrible Beothuk massacre of unprecedented scale. Although history is vague on the facts, and the numbers may have possibly been exaggerated, there are those who still relate the story with conviction.

For information on Terry's published books as well as future books, please take a moment to "like" and follow Terry Foss Author Facebook page or visit Terry's website shown below.

Website: www.terryfoss.ca

Email: terryfoss@nf.sympatico.ca

Facebook: facebook.com/terryfossauthor

Distribution: www.shopdownhome.com

Made in the USA
Monee, IL
10 October 2020